MISADVENTURES

WITH A

LAWYER

MISADVENTURES
WITH A
LAWYER

BY
JULIE MORGAN

WATERHOUSE PRESS

Heather, Martha, and Christina —
you're like a trifecta of amazingness.
Thank you for the support and love.

CHAPTER ONE

AINSLEY

On Friday, I woke with excitement for Ashley's wedding. My best friend since childhood, she of course had asked me to be one of her bridesmaids, and I couldn't wait to get the weekend started.

Today, we had a full schedule of hair and nail appointments and other fun plans before the rehearsal dinner tonight. It was time to get my bridesmaid duty on.

I bounced out of bed toward the kitchen as my phone rang. I predicted it to be Ashley, but instead it was Amy, our law firm's receptionist.

"Hi, Ainsley," she said.

"Hi," I answered, trying to hide my apprehension about why she was calling me.

"Mr. Newstrom is wondering when he should expect you at the office."

"But I'm supposed to be off today," I told her.

"Well, according to him, you're still working on Mr. Vanderbilt's case, and you're expected to be at the office and, shortly after that, court."

She wasn't short or curt, but she got her point across.

Chase Newstrom, my boss and the owner of the law firm I worked for, knew I had a full weekend of wedding plans with my best friend. I had it on both of our calendars. He had said he had no issue with me taking Friday off, yet here we were, with me expected to work after all.

"Thanks, Amy," I mumbled. "I'll be there in an hour." And I hung up.

It hurt like hell that he didn't care about plans I'd made for my own personal time and he'd had the receptionist call to break the news. Should he have cared about what I had been planning to do? No, not necessarily, but what if it were something important like surgery? I couldn't have canceled that just because he needed me in the office.

This wasn't surgery, though, nor my wedding. *Thank goodness.* I was so not ready for that.

I phoned Ashley and the other bridesmaids and broke the bad news about not being able to join them for the hair and nail appointments. Ashley wasn't happy. In fact, she said she'd disown me if I skipped any of the other wedding events.

I would disown me as a friend too.

♦ ♦ ♦ ♦

Sitting.

Waiting.

Anticipating.

These three words have become my life. *Good things come to those who wait?* What a lie. Whoever came up with that didn't understand law students waiting for their bar exam results *or* a girl wanting to meet up with her best friend on the eve of her wedding.

I knew from the moment I was a little girl that I wanted to be an attorney. I wanted to stand up for those who had no voice, to help victims of crimes who could not help themselves. Our professors had always encouraged us to follow our passion, so it was a surprise when I had sat in on my first court hearing and realized prosecution might not be for me. Instead, it was defense.

Surprisingly, I found many cases were tried where the defendant was actually innocent. They needed someone to hear their side of the story and fight their fight. That was where I wanted to stand, next to the falsely accused.

It was the middle of May in Dallas, Texas. The sun made it feel like we were in Satan's backyard while he grilled dogs and invited the demons and hellspawn over for sweet tea. It felt so hot that I wondered if one could potentially cook bacon on the sidewalk—not that I'd ever try that, of course.

I was thankful to be spending the day in the air conditioning of the courthouse, even if I wished I were somewhere else entirely. Still, this was my professional passion, so things could be worse.

The law firm I was working for—until my exam results came through—represented many of the high court cases. Rich, deep pockets crossed our threshold and often said, "Money is no object." They demanded our representation, and they received it . . . most of the time.

Alleged crooked politicians, extortionists, and financial advisors who stole money from their clients—we represented them all. The only clients our firm would turn away were cases having to deal with serial killers, serial rapists, and abuse of children. If the evidence was enough to prove innocence, however, the firm would consider the case. More often than not, though, there were some lines even we wouldn't cross.

The courthouse atmosphere was chilly inside, and that

wasn't from the air conditioning. The judge looked bored. His eyes were half-hooded, and he rested his chin on his hand. I picked at the corner of my binder, where one day it would hold my own business cards, which would say *Ainsley Speire - Attorney at Law.*

I'd looked forward to this day since I was a little girl. I loved a good debate and would argue until my face turned blue. The only thing on the walls of my small office was my law degree from the University of Texas. My father had it framed a bit larger than it needed to be, and it took up much more wall space than it needed to. I didn't care. I loved it.

I turned through the notes in my binder. Everything was leading toward a win for us. It was a matter of time before the prosecution rested their case and we took over and wrapped it up.

That was where Chase Newstrom, lawyer extraordinaire, always came in. He seldom lost a case, and as a defense attorney, that was a golden flag one would want to fly at the top of their pole.

He sat back in his chair and pressed the tips of his fingers together like a steeple. They rested against the tip of his nose, his thumbs pressed against his chin. His dark-brown hair was styled perfectly, his lashes long and thick, and his baby-blue eyes stared straight at the back of the city attorney's head.

Chase was a beautiful man, and he knew it. He'd done a photoshoot for his firm, and I was honestly curious when *GQ* would come knocking on his door. Women hung on to every word he spoke, though more than half had no idea what the man was talking about. He was a tour de force of masculinity and brooding good looks. He was a successful defense attorney, wealthy, and had the beauty of a fallen angel and body of a Greek god.

Hell, beautiful didn't describe him. I could have easily drooled over the man, but he had no idea who I was, other than an intern hoping to make a career for herself. I suppose I should feel fortunate he took me on, and I *am* grateful, but what I wouldn't give for five minutes with the man.

While he was at the office, he was clean-shaven and took his appearance seriously. The man wore top-of-the-line clothing attire, whereas I bought my dresses and pantsuits from stores like Ross and Marshalls. It was what I could afford. Chase had every article of clothing custom-tailored to him, while with some of mine, the waist was too big or the pant legs or skirts were too long. I dreamed of the day I'd be able to have custom-tailored clothes.

Doubtful, but a woman could dream.

"Never miss a chance to make a perfect first impression" was one of the first things he said to me during my interview, while he took in my choice of clothes. He didn't undress me with his eyes, though. He was more or less judging me for my lack of fashion sense. But I was here to hopefully practice law, not make a fashion statement.

I closed my eyes and thought about all the delicious things I would do to him and how he would ruin me for anyone else. I cleared my throat and opened my eyes once more to try to focus on the case instead of the scent of his cologne. It hypnotized me. I could bathe in it.

Some of the women I had seen coming and going through the office looked as if they were models who had just stepped off the runway. Tall and very slender with clothes that flowed from their toothpick bodies. Some were clearly fake and took an interest in Chase just because of his looks and money. It was sad, really. They reminded me of marionette dolls on strings, puppeted by an ego so thick they couldn't see the idiocy of their own being.

The song from *Pinocchio* about having no strings to hold him down played through my mind.

I giggled at myself and hummed the tune in my head.

Then there was me. I was an average woman with a typical body. I wasn't rail thin, but I was proportionate.

In the early morning hours, I would sometimes catch Chase after he finished up at the gym. He would come in with his workout clothes on, his gym shirt stuck to his sweat-covered chest and back and the shadow of the previous day's growth on his cheeks and chin. I would try not to stare, but I couldn't help myself. If he was facing me, his shorts were sometimes fitted, and the outline of his cock... He was well packaged. The man was a god among men. And he had no idea I even existed.

Did he know I'd just taken the bar exam? Did he know I wanted to work in his office if I passed? Would he let me stay once I was certified? Would he help mold my career?

Did he realize I hung on every single word he muttered?

These were questions that would, in time, one way or the other, be answered. For now, I was content learning and listening to as much as he'd allow.

The client we were representing was Lance Vanderbilt, the starting quarterback for his college. His family donated large sums of money to multiple charities annually, and he had scouts after him, as he was assured to go pro. He had his whole life ahead of him but stood accused of raping Miranda Cooper, an acquaintance of his.

Lance groaned in what sounded like boredom.

I glanced at the six-foot-four, light-blond-haired, tanned-skinned quarterback and found him slouched in his chair, arms crossed over his chest, his left leg bouncing in a nervous twitch.

I reached over the spectator wall and tapped his shoulder. He turned and looked at me, then rolled his eyes.

"What's your problem?" I whispered to Lance.

"When will this be over?" he asked. "I didn't do it, and I want to go home."

"Give Mr. Newstrom the time to win your case, and you'll be home before you know it. Now, please, be quiet, sit up straight, and stop yawning."

"I'm trying," he whispered back as he sat up.

The judge looked over to us and frowned.

I sat back in my seat and watched as Chase stood to begin his part of the question-and-answer session. He paced back and forth as he questioned the witness, Joy Anderson, who was a friend of the accuser. She was pretty in a girl-next-door sort of way.

I thought back to the conversation we'd had with Lance during our initial interview.

"Did you have sex with her?" Chase asked him.

Lance nodded. "Yes, on a number of occasions. We were very close. I don't understand why she would say I raped her. It was never like that."

"Why would she do this now?" I asked. "What would be her motive?"

Chase looked to me and then to Lance. "Your family is quite wealthy, are they not?"

Lance nodded. "Yeah, my dad comes from money. He didn't want me dating Miranda because she was poor and from the wrong side of the tracks."

"What is that supposed to mean?" I asked.

Chase sat back in his seat and crossed his arms over his chest. He lifted his brow and gave me a look that said are you serious.

I frowned and gave my attention back to Lance.

"Her family is dirt poor," Chase said. "Dad told me if I didn't watch myself and cover my shit, I could get her pregnant, and then her family would come after us for money. But I always used protection." Lance shook his head. "My dad said she was a 'gold-digging whore.' I never thought she'd ever do that. She seemed so honest. I never saw this coming."

I refocused my attention to listen to Chase grill Joy Anderson.

"Is it true, Miss Anderson, that you did not see the plaintiff, Miss Miranda Cooper, until two days after she accused my client of rape?"

"Correct," Joy answered.

"Then help me and the court understand, Miss Anderson, how you claim to have witnessed the rape, but you were not with the plaintiff until two days later."

"Well, I wasn't exactly in the room—"

"Objection!" yelled the prosecuting attorney.

"Overruled," the judge ordered. "Continue with your questioning, Mr. Newstrom."

"Thank you, Your Honor," Chase said. "Please, Miss Anderson, state for the court, if you would, that you were not in the room, nor did you witness the rape of the plaintiff, Miss Miranda Cooper."

I watched the witness sink in her chair in defeat. I was positive she was praying for the floor to open up and swallow her. If you lie on the stand, you could be charged with perjury.

Your testimony would be dismissed, and the case for the plaintiff would look questionable.

"I... I was not there, no. But—"

"Thank you. Your Honor, I'm done with this witness," Chase said and turned his back on Joy Anderson.

"You may step down," the judge said.

Joy stood, and a tear slid down her cheek. *I'm sorry,* she mouthed toward her friend Miranda. She looked over to our witness, Lance Vanderbilt. "You're a fucking dirtbag who deserves to die for what you did!"

"You will be held in contempt if you speak another word, Miss Anderson," the judge ordered. "Do you understand?"

I glanced over to Chase and found him smirking. This wasn't quite what he had wanted, but the fact that the woman was accusing Lance of lying when it was she who lied was enough to dismiss the charges.

Maybe.

"The jury will dismiss this outburst from the witness, and the reporter will strike the statement from the record," the judge instructed.

Chase had told Lance early on he would not put him on the stand. He wanted to break down the witness and her stories—her lies. So far, it was working. I glanced at Miranda, and she squirmed in her chair.

According to Lance, no rape had ever happened. He had an account of his time with her, and that was up to Chase to present as evidence.

In comes Miranda Cooper, beautiful and with a shy demeanor. She came from a poor family, her brother had been in and out of jail for drugs, her father was nonexistent, and her mother had boyfriends turn over more often than riders of Greyhound.

Lance had been attracted to Miranda, as apparently she had been to him. The two had dated for a while, and one night he'd taken her to a frat party. He'd kept her by his side the entire night and watched what she drank. Too many college girls were roofied and taken advantage of. But not Miranda, and definitely not by Lance.

The night was in full swing, and Miranda Cooper wanted to have sex. She came on to Lance and seduced him to take her up into one of the bedrooms. Lance had used protection.

Fast forward two days later, Miranda claimed she was raped by Lance.

At first, Lance claimed he didn't understand what was happening, that Miranda was his girlfriend and he'd never rape her or force her to do anything she didn't want to do. But the accusations continued.

Lance's parents reached out immediately to Chase for legal assistance and hired him and his team.

Almost a year later, here we were in court over a *he said, she said* court case. All of the discovery had been covered, and nothing new had been presented.

Until today.

"Your Honor, I have a new witness who will prove the forceful rape of my client, Miss Miranda Cooper."

Chase frowned and stood. "Objection, Your Honor. This evidence has not been presented in discovery."

The judge shook his head and glared at the prosecution. "I should dismiss this case for the lack of integrity on your part as a prosecutor." The judge picked up his anvil. "The evidence will be shared and reviewed. We'll recess for the weekend and return to continue then."

I leaned forward to Lance. "Just three days and this is over," I reminded him.

"Three days too long, Chase," he said to my boss. "I didn't rape her."

"I know you didn't. We'll get you off. Don't worry." Chase closed his briefcase.

What the hell evidence did the prosecution have that we weren't already aware of? My gut told me Miranda's mother was behind the accusations. She wanted a payout, and in court today, she was here wearing a designer outfit that her salary couldn't afford. Considering the payout she'd be expecting on Miranda's behalf, I wondered how much of this was her doing.

Did I think Lance was guilty? No, I didn't. Did we think Miranda's family was after a payout? Absolutely. They'd offered to settle out of court, but settling would show a sign of guilt, and well, Lance was not guilty.

And it was up to Chase Newstrom to prove that.

And he would. He always did.

CHAPTER TWO

CHASE

Signed, sealed, and delivered. That was what I had expected when I woke this morning. A clean-cut case of an innocent man who had been accused of a heinous act he had not committed. At least that was what I had thought before the prosecutor moved to introduce new evidence.

As defense attorneys, we had the right to review the evidence disclosed. The defense was entitled to know about the prosecution's case before trial and vice versa. Nothing was kept as a secret. We had ample opportunity to study all sides of the case. Our side, their side, and, somewhere in the middle, the truth. To pull this crap toward the end of their case was not only wrong, but it could potentially cause the case to be thrown out. No one wanted to start over, but if it meant a win for my team and me, we'd take it.

I could always hope, but we'd review this new evidence regardless. As lawyers, it was what we did, and Lance would be a free man soon.

The prosecution had offered a plea deal, which we'd refused. Admit guilt, and the sentence would be a year in jail with four years' probation. If my client were actually guilty, it would be a great plea, but my client was innocent. We promptly gave them a "hell no," followed by, "see you in court."

They'd better hold on to hope that once this was over, we wouldn't slap the family with a countersuit.

As soon as Ainsley and I entered my office building, I closed the doors behind us. The only sound was the hum of the air conditioner. It was late afternoon on a Friday, and soon the sun would set. Everyone else in the office had their door closed or was off having a glass of something other than water.

Tonight was supposed to end in victory. Instead, it ended with me back here, trying to figure out what went wrong.

"Did you know about this witness?" I asked Ainsley Speire, my intern. She wore a black dress, and her auburn hair was braided to the side. She was a plain-Jane kind of woman with curves. She was stacked and attractive but not the type I'd normally go for.

I didn't even know if I had a type, but the women on my arm were typically models or someone equally successful as me. I didn't date other lawyers. It ended badly, at least in my experience.

Ainsley shook her head. "No, sir, I didn't. I know as much as you do at the moment."

"Well, it's your job to make sure shit like this doesn't happen."

I hated surprises. Don't sneak up on me with anything, and we'd be just fine. But if you hit me with something in court that I had not been privy to? It was a sure way to get your ass spanked by the hand of the law. I took what I did very seriously, and if anyone fucked with that or got in my way, I'd mow them over before they realized anything had happened.

Ainsley took a seat at the table in my office and opened her briefcase. She hadn't responded to my statement, which was fine. I argued for a living, but I didn't necessarily want to fight with my own staff. I didn't feel the need to show her where she was wrong and how to fix it. If I did that for her every time she fucked up, how would she learn?

Did she fuck up? No, not necessarily, but I had relied on her to prepare everything I needed for this case. If she wanted this to be her career, she needed to learn the ropes and learn them the hard way, like I had. If everything was always given to you, how would you ever learn? You wouldn't, at least not in my corner of the world. You busted your ass for what you wanted, whether for your career or for personal gains.

With a sigh, I removed my jacket and tie, unbuttoned the first two buttons of my dress shirt, and rolled my sleeves up to midforearm.

I pulled out a chair from the table and took a seat. "Who the hell is this new witness?" I met Ainsley's gaze and found her staring at me. I frowned. "What is it?"

She quickly shook her head, and a blush crept to her cheeks. She cleared her throat and started talking. "I'm reading over his information now. Please, just a moment so I can finish?"

"Fine," I mumbled, crossing my arms over my chest and then pinching the bridge of my nose. I glanced over to Ainsley and found her watching me again. "Seriously, what is it?"

"Oh," she said, startled, and she looked back down to the documents in front of her. The blush on her cheeks darkened. "I figured," she started in a soft, mouselike voice, "since you were getting comfortable, I might remove my shoes. My feet hurt."

I shrugged. "Do whatever you need to do. We need to get this shit settled." My phone buzzed in my pocket, and I pulled it out with a sigh. "Shit," I growled and sat back in my chair.

"Everything okay?" Ainsley asked.

I raised my brows and then cocked my head to the side and looked at her. "Yeah, it's fine. Just forgot I had something to do tonight." More like some*one*, but Ainsley didn't need to know that.

I had a date with a model. We had been seeing each other for a few months now, but by *seeing*, it was no more than her showing up at my place, me fucking her, and then her leaving. We laughed at each other's jokes and pretended we were interested, but it was nothing more than sex. She was taking off for London soon. Maybe tonight would be her farewell fuck-off. I smirked at my own thoughts.

"Yeah, I have something—"

"Did you find what you were looking for?" I asked at the same time.

Ainsley cleared her throat. "Umm"—she paused to look at me and then back to the papers—"sort of. Someone has stated they witnessed the rape by peeking into the room while it was happening."

I guffawed at her findings. "Bullshit. Who was it?"

"I'm looking into it." She wrote something down on her paper. "I'll get you a name soon."

"So you have this handled, then?" I asked and stood from my chair. My phone buzzed again, and I shoved it into my pocket. My date would have to wait. They said patience was a virtue, although with her, it appeared to have run off with her virginity.

Ainsley looked up at me as if I had asked her a question in a foreign language.

"Well, I did have plans tonight," she said.

"You're going to have to change them. Welcome to the

world of being a defense attorney, Ainsley." I pulled my keys from my pocket and tapped my desk. "There's a set of keys in the top drawer to lock up. I expect you to find out what you can about this new key witness before you head home. Or take it home with you. Doesn't matter to me. Just get it done. Understood? We'll meet back here tomorrow morning to review your findings."

She looked down at the stack of folders and files in front of her. With a sigh, she nodded. "Yes, sir."

I stepped past her and opened my office door before glancing over my shoulder at the young woman in my office. She had the world ahead of her. She would appreciate this one day. Maybe not tonight or this weekend, but if she wanted to continue working here, to get ahead in this field and get a letter of recommendation from me, then she would do what needed to be done.

As for me, I had a beautiful woman waiting. No relationship crap, just sex, booze, and maybe a cigar when we finished.

I thought about my older brother. He was married and had three kids, two boys and a girl. "One day you're going to meet a woman who will knock you on your ass, and you won't know which way is up," he'd said once. "And I want to be there when it happens!"

Not today, brother, or any other day. Fuck being someone's other half. I didn't have time for that crap.

I climbed in behind the wheel of my Audi and sped down the road toward my home. I glanced in the rearview mirror and watched my office building grow smaller and smaller the more distance I put between us.

Monday, we would walk into the courthouse, ready to

put this case to bed and free my client. This would be the last weekend Lance had to spend any time behind bars. As soon as he was released, my cleanup team would work with him to help clear his name. Even if found innocent, his name had still been dragged through the mud. Half the battle was the case. The other was clearing his name and making sure he still had his scholarships.

I glanced in the rearview mirror again and looked at my own reflection. Sometimes I was asked how I could sleep, knowing the criminals I defended. I would smile and say, "With my eyes closed."

A story is only as good as its villain is a quote by Luke Taylor I used often. If you had a bad villain, the story would suck. If there was no villain, then you had no story.

I supposed in a way that made me the narrator of villains' stories. But so long as I was paid and knew the truth, I was good with the decisions I'd made.

However, there were some cases I would not touch, and for good reason. Murder, child abuse, rape… If I had a suspicion the accused was actually guilty, hell to the no. Go get yourself a court-appointed lawyer.

With a smirk, I continued my drive and turned down the road that led to my condo. I pulled in, and a silhouette inside the guard shack moved in my direction. He stepped out and nodded to me with a tilt of his hat.

"Good evening, Mr. Newstrom."

"Good evening, Baxter. How's your mom?"

Baxter was the resident guard who kept our grounds safe. He was somewhere in his mid-forties to fifties and took care of his mom.

"She's good, Mr. Newstrom, a spitfire." He chuckled and

opened the gate with the push of a button. "Enjoy your night, sir. Oh, and a lovely young lady came calling. She was let inside. I had her on your list."

"Ahh, yes, thank you, Baxter. Enjoy your night."

I pulled through the entrance and turned right, and just outside my garage stood a long, lean, and tanned woman with blond hair to her midback. She wore a red fitted dress that hugged her thighs.

I rolled down my passenger window and leaned over. "Thanks for waiting for me, Ginger." I pressed the garage door button, and it began to lift up.

"No problem, Chase. I'll follow you inside."

And just like that, my night began to look up. Ginger—she preferred to be called by her stage name—never gave me a hard time about being late. I opened my car door, and her heels struck the concrete as she approached.

"Long day at the office?" she asked.

"Long day at the courthouse, but enough about that." I closed the car door behind me and pulled her into my arms. I slanted my lips across hers, and Ginger leaned her body against mine. "Inside. Now," I ordered, and everything about today washed away.

She took my inner elbow with her hand, and we walked through my open garage. The faint lighting illuminated Ginger's white-blond hair, almost in a glow.

I opened the door and let her inside first, then closed it behind me. Taking her hand, I pulled her back toward me and wrapped my arms around her body. I grabbed one of her legs and lifted it up around my waist and then followed with her other leg. She hugged my waist tight with her thighs, and I pressed the fob remote to close the garage door.

The events of today were already far from my mind, and I was ready to settle down for the evening inside Ginger. Later, maybe a glass of Scotch.

CHAPTER THREE

AINSLEY

Chase gave no fucks except about himself. If I were more like him, if I had stood up to him and said, "No, I can't be there today," he would have fired me. He didn't take lightly to anyone second-guessing him or standing up to voice an opinion different from his.

Instead, I was always the "yes sir" girl of the office. I wanted to build a reputation for becoming a ball-busting lawyer, but I'd get nowhere if I continued saying yes to everything and being everywhere he expected regardless of any plans of mine. It made me feel like that girl who disowned her friends as soon as a guy took interest in her. That had never been me.

Chase came and went and expected me to do all this work for him. I had busted my ass at his firm, but I still felt like he didn't take me seriously.

"Pay your dues, Ainsley," he'd said on more than one occasion, "and one day, this could be you ordering someone else around."

Well, maybe I didn't want to order someone around like he did. Maybe I wanted someone to work *with* me, not for me or under me. It wasn't nice how he treated people, and the fact that I was missing the pre-wedding events with my friends made me hate him that much more.

Not long after Chase left me here in the office, I actually did find where this new witness had been, and it was nowhere near the house party the night Lance was accused of rape. Social media had been a godsend in many aspects of my job.

He had been across the country with his family. After searching a few of the databases we had of flight information and car rentals, his name came up. He had been in a different state during the party. I found his social media pages full of pictures of Miranda and him. Were they lovers? It wasn't our business, unless it helped get our client off.

We'd make damn sure they both paid for this lie. Who was this guy trying to cover for? Was he promised money? It wouldn't surprise me. The accuser's family was poor, and I could empathize, but going after someone who had money wasn't the way to get ahead.

Miranda and her fellow witnesses could be found guilty of perjury, Lance's parents could countersue, and Miranda could serve time in jail for slander and defamation of character. There was a world of shit they'd all go through if Lance's family had any say in it. His family lawyered up, and Miranda's team honestly didn't stand a chance.

This evidence would have the new "witness's" testimony thrown out before it was even heard. Did the prosecution do no homework? This was ridiculous. Chase would eat this boy alive if he did testify. He would then turn the tables on the family and rake them through the coals and make sure they burned.

But right now, tonight, it was about me being pissed the fuck off at Chase. He could thank me later for the detective work I did. It wasn't like it was hard. It was easy. Almost too easy. The prosecution seriously was a joke in this case, and it was disappointing.

I looked at the clock. It was closing in on midnight. I groaned in disappointment at myself. I sat back in my chair, and my head lolled back and rested on the headrest. I closed my eyes and let out a long sigh. The longer I sat there, the more the rage continued to rise. I gritted my teeth and opened my eyes. I fisted my hands and then howled in frustration.

"Who the hell does he think he is?" I said out loud. "With his Gucci shoes and Armani blazer?" I stood and pushed the chair back with my legs. "His amazing cologne that makes me feel dumb because I can't think around him?"

I pushed away from the table and placed my fists on my hips. While he was off gallivanting around town, I was stuck here missing the wedding rehearsal. The bride would never forgive me if I didn't show up tomorrow. The wedding was so important. I had to be there, no matter what. Chase had to understand that.

One of the walls of his office was lined with shelves of law books. Another wall held his credentials from Harvard Law, University of North Texas, and a few of the recognitions he'd received from the charity work he did.

Across the room, next to one of the framed plaques, I spied his liquor cabinet. I made a beeline for it and opened the panel. Inside was expensive Scotch, brandy, and who knew what else. They were all brown liquid, and I wasn't picky. I wasn't what you'd call an expensive drinker. If you gave me a beer, I was good.

However, I knew Scotch was pricy, and what better way to get back at my douchebag of a boss than by drinking his most favorite spirit?

I grabbed a glass and pulled the top off the crystal bottle that held the brown contents. Both probably cost more than two years of my current intern salary. I poured myself a glass and then brought it to my lips. I sniffed the contents and cringed. Scotch was strong, yet so was brandy. I had tasted brandy once. I wasn't a fan. Hopefully I liked the Scotch, because I planned to drink a lot of it tonight.

"Fucking asshole," I said and sipped the contents. When I swallowed, I growled with the burning sensation as the contents slipped down my throat. Surprisingly, it warmed my belly in a delightful way. "Not so bad," I said to myself and took another sip. Then another and another. Before I realized it, I had to refill my glass.

"I hate my boss. I hate him!" I looked at one of his pictures, where he was shaking hands with the governor of Texas. I pointed at it. "I hate you, Chase Newstrom!"

I took another drink and then held my arms straight up, as if I were cheering for myself. In a way, I was. "You are the world's worst boss and biggest asshole I have ever come across!" I then giggled at my words. "Well, you personally have never made me come, but damn, have I had some erotic dreams about you."

I laughed once more and then shook off the erotic notions of Chase. He had been a dick tonight, and I would not give in to the pleasure of anything erotic in his name. What if he had plans and I had insisted he stayed? Oh, that's right, he did have plans. Well, boo-fucking-hoo.

"Get your knob blown and come back in here and help a girl out!" The Scotch was starting to work its magic, and I was feeling quite woozy. And woozy felt delightful. My body warmed, and my skin flushed from the liquor.

"You know what you need, Mr. Newstrom? You need a swift kick in your ass!" I grabbed the bottle of Scotch, crossed the room back to his desk, and then kicked his chair. It spun toward me, and I took a seat in it. The leather was cool to my body, and for a moment, I relished in it.

I kicked off my shoes and poured more liquor into my glass. I took another sip and stared down at the personalized letterhead notepad on his desk. Next to it was a quill he said he brought back from Venice.

I smirked. Tonight called for a note. No, a letter. The letter of all letters to the world's worst but sexiest boss.

Dear Mr. Chase Newstrom—

I drew out a long line after his name and then tapped the pen on the paper.

You, sir, are an asshole. Not just any asshole, mind you, the world's biggest asshole. Your asshole is so big that it would take the world's largest tampon to seal you over. You have no idea what you did tonight, nor do you actually care. Which is a problem. The world is not about you, it doesn't revolve around you, and if you took a minute to smell the fucking roses, you'd see there was life revolving AROUND you.

I took another sip of Scotch and licked the residue off my upper lip. I decided I really liked Scotch. I wasn't sure how much this liquor was, but I knew it would be a shame to let it go later when I would need to pee. I continued with my hate mail.

I had a wedding to attend this weekend, and thanks to you,

I now have to skip it.

Thanks to you, my friends will never forgive me. Thanks to you, my friend, who is the bride, will most likely kill me. Thanks to you, my parents will disown me for putting my job first. Thanks to you, I'll be the laughingstock of my friendship circle. Well, the circle I had, which is completely gone now, so thanks for that.

I paused and took another sip of Scotch. My eyes grew blurry as the words spilled out of me.

You walk in here with that tight ass of yours, in your designer clothes, and you smell so good. Even the days you come in with your workout clothes on. The sweaty clothes cling to your body like some sort of drive-me-crazy carnal paint. You take my breath away when you step into a room. Your eyes seduce me in ways that only my erotic dreams can handle. You make me weak in the knees, and I can't look at you longer than a few minutes for fear of lunging into your arms.

And if given a chance, I would ruin you for any other woman. I would do things to you you've never experienced with anyone else. Hell, I would let you ruin me for any other man.

I wasn't sure what I would do that was so miraculous, but damn it, I would definitely go down trying!

I find myself longing for you, wondering what you would feel like inside me, to have you on top of me, or your face between my legs. I close my eyes and fantasize about seducing you, straddling your body and claiming you as my own. There have been many nights I wanted to tell you how I felt, but you barely even know I exist. It hurts so much to know there's something you want so desperately but no matter what you do, you'll never have it. Much less deserve it.

But I do deserve it, Chase. I deserve the world and so much more. I've worked my ass off to get to where I am today. So maybe the joke's on you. So why don't you take your tight ass and your well-built body I could bounce a quarter off of and go to hell. Go jerk off to whatever woman is floating your boat this week. I'll pray for you that your dick doesn't shrivel up and fall off!

I drank down the rest of my Scotch and poured what was left of the liquor into my glass.

And no, I'm not going to buy you more booze. So go fuck yourself, Chase! Because you'll never get the chance to fuck me. I would have gladly bent over your desk and let you touch me. I would never commit that type of fuck-and-run with anyone else, but with you, I would.

But not now. Not ever. That ship has fucking sailed!

Never to be yours . . .

Ainsley Speire

After I signed my name to the letter, I swallowed back the contents of my glass and slammed the glass down. I licked the Scotch and ran my hand over the note I wrote. I nodded to myself and smiled, proud of what I'd written.

"I'll show him who's in charge here," I said with a hiccup.

I swiped my arm across my mouth and laid my head down on my arms. I closed and opened my eyelids slowly, as if I were in slow motion. I was tired and needed a nap. Maybe all of this was a dream. I mean, after all, I would never in a million years have written a letter like that to my boss.

No fucking way. He would have absolutely fired me.

I would just tear it up later. He would never have to know.

Intending to close my eyes just long enough to burn through the liquor, I felt myself drift off into fantasies of Chase.

My favorite one was him holding my body against the wall. He held my wrists above my head while he kissed me. He pressed his knees between my thighs and his erection against the heated folds of my pussy.

He would move his hands over my body, massaging my full breasts and teasing my nipples through my bra. I needed him as much as he needed me, but before I could tell him the words, "fuck me," darkness took me under completely and I faded into the oblivion.

CHAPTER FOUR

CHASE

Saturdays were meant to be spent on ourselves, doing things like going to the gym, catching up on laundry, and watching college football. I worked all week so I could enjoy the weekends, yet here I was again driving to the office on a Saturday.

I spent countless hours running my practice. Empires weren't built overnight, after all. Running a successful law firm meant long hours and, sometimes, blood, sweat, and tears. I was no one's bitch when it came to law, and I damn well wasn't going to work for someone else. I was too much a hard-ass and too confident in my own abilities.

As the doors to the elevator opened to my floor, I prepared myself to review the notes Ainsley would have left me regarding any information and evidence she had found. I would then prepare what I needed for Monday, with her assistance whenever she decided to show up, and then we'd reconvene in court on Monday and prove Lance's innocence. Bam, done. Celebrate and get laid.

I stepped out into the bright open area of the empty reception of my firm's office, again appreciating the cleanliness. First impressions were important. Some of my clients might be shady, but it didn't mean my office had to be.

To maintain a pristine environment, I expected a lot—or maybe more accurately, nothing—from my staff. Don't bring your problems to work. And don't wallpaper anything with photos of your family. My employees were here to do a job, not take away from the professional environment by posting pictures of dogs, cats, and however many kids they had.

I loved my family and my niece and nephews, sure, but no one would find their pictures plastered anywhere in my office. Some called me a cold, callous asshole, but if that helped me win my battles, then I was all for it.

When I pushed my key into my personal office door, surprise rolled through me to find it unlocked.

What the hell? Did Ainsley forget to lock my door?

Upon opening it and entering my office, my senses were assaulted by the strong scent of...*Scotch?* I frowned and looked around the room. Piles of papers were stacked here and there, and food containers littered my table. And there, head down on my desk, was a passed-out Ainsley Speire.

In one hand she held a glass with just about enough liquor left for a shot. In the other, she held the quill pen I had brought back from a trip to Venice. Next to her was my most expensive bottle of Scotch, completely drained. And partially tucked between her arm and the desk was a handwritten note of some sort.

Everything I loathed about dirtiness crept over my skin like a centipede on a leaf. A growl erupted from Ainsley, and I frowned. *Was that a snore?*

Her hair fell in tendrils over her face, and she looked peaceful. I moved a few strands of her hair, and repugnance pulled at my lips. She had been drooling.

On my desk. *Perfect.*

I moved her hand, causing the pen to fall to the floor, and then I pulled the paper out from under her arm and held it up.

"Dear Mr. Chase Newstrom," I started out loud.

Maybe Ainsley would wake before I got to the end. I lifted my brow and adjusted my stance. I glanced down at her and then continued to read while she slept off the booze.

"You, sir, are an asshole." I paused and looked down at her again. "Asshole, huh?"

I returned to the letter and read to myself about the wedding events she had planned to attend starting yesterday.

Shit. I forgot about her wedding plans. *Okay, I may be an asshole.* Well, she could have reminded me, so really, whose fault was it?

"Thanks to you, my friends will never forgive me." I snorted. "Yeah, whatever. Your friends will get over it." I skimmed down until the word *ass* grabbed my attention.

> *You walk in here with that tight ass of yours, in your designer clothes, and you smell so good. Even the days you come in with your workout clothes on. The sweaty clothes cling to your body like some sort of drive-me-crazy carnal paint.*

This last part made me chuckle. I continued reading to myself.

> *You take my breath away when you step into a room.*

I paused and looked down at Ainsley. Had she always felt this way? How had I not seen it? I turned my back to her and paced the room as I read.

Your eyes seduce me in ways that only my erotic dreams can handle. You make me weak in the knees, and I can't look at you longer than a few minutes for fear of lunging into your arms.

I stopped once more. I'd had staff members crush on me before but not quite like this. I continued her letter until the end and then paced until I heard movement from the desk.

I turned to face a waking Ainsley slowly rising from her slumber. I glanced down at the letter and read a choice excerpt.

"So maybe the joke's on you. Why don't you take your tight ass and your well-built body I could bounce a quarter off of and go to hell. Go jerk off to whatever woman is floating your boat this week. I'll pray for you that your dick doesn't shrivel up and fall off! And no, I'm not going to buy you more booze. So go fuck yourself, Chase, because you'll never get the chance to fuck me. I would have gladly bent over your desk, but that ship has fucking sailed! Never to be yours." I paused and met her gaze. "Ainsley Speire."

I folded the note, smirked, and took a step forward.

She looked down and slowly swiped her sleeve across the drool she'd left behind.

"I—" A blush crept up her neck to her cheeks.

"Nice letter," I said and took another step toward her. "Did you enjoy my Scotch?"

Her skin flushed further with a bright shade of red. "I'm sorry," she whispered.

"No, you're not. If you were sorry, you wouldn't have raided my liquor cabinet."

"Am I fired?" she asked.

Ainsley met my gaze once more and bit her bottom lip.

Her shirt was disheveled. It was what she had worn the day before, and the first few buttons were open. The top of her breasts barely crested the material, but it was enough to send a thrill of erotic thoughts through my mind.

How had I not seen Ainsley like this before? Yes, she was a woman, but I'd never seen her as anything but an employee. She had just taken her bar exam, and I guessed a part of me had looked at her as someone green, someone who knew nothing about nothing, and I liked my women smart. I wanted someone who understood their body and knew how to use it, not someone new to sex who had no idea what it meant to be sexy.

Was this the real Ainsley? Was I only now seeing her for the first time?

"We will see, Ms. Speire," I finally answered. "We will see. But I promise you I am intrigued by this little note of yours."

"I'm so sorry," she mumbled. "Oh, shit." She quickly held her hand over her mouth.

I chuckled. "Do I need to read this to you again?" I held it up, and her skin flushed crimson once more. If she didn't watch herself, she would have no blood left throughout the rest of her body. "It's quite eye-opening, you know?"

"Mr. Newstrom, I didn't mean... What I mean to say is... I'm sorry. I just... well? My friends—"

"I could give a rat's ass about your friends. You are here to work for me and earn your stripes. You want to be a part of a successful law firm? This is how you get shit done. You stay the extra hours. You do the research. You expect the unexpected, and you prepare for it." I held the letter up once more. "However, I didn't expect this from you."

She held her face in her hands and remained seated in my chair. "I'm sorry. I'm so sorry." She wiped at her face, and her makeup from yesterday smeared across her cheeks.

Ahh hell, she was crying. I hated it when women cried. I was a hard-ass, but I did have a soft spot for women I may have made cry. Unless they deserved it, but that was a totally different topic.

"Ainsley, look," I said and stepped behind my desk. I crouched down in front of her to try again. "I do not apologize for making you stay late. However, I am sorry you missed your friend's wedding. That was a jackhole thing for me to do. If you had told me, reminded me, I would have understood and let you go."

"What?" she asked. "You would have let me go if I had reminded you?" She sat back in the chair and shook her head. "I think I'm pretty much fired here, so I'm just going to say what's on my mind."

"I haven't said that," I reminded her.

"I reminded you all week about my best friend's wedding. I had reminders on your calendar and mine. I even mentioned something about it during the court case this week. I'm a bridesmaid, and I didn't even show up for the rehearsal. I canceled my hair and nail appointments with her, and if I'm lucky, she'll still let me stand for her. But I can't expect to be there if I'm here. I was here working for you while you decided to go out on a date. So yes, Mr. Newstrom, I drank your Scotch."

She stood from the chair and paced the room.

I stood to full height and set the letter on the table. I felt like the worst boss ever. With a sigh, I motioned to the paperwork. "Why don't we do a quick review of what you found last night?"

She rubbed her head and stood in the middle of the room. "I need a shower, to brush my teeth, and maybe throw up. Not all in that order."

I opened my desk drawer and then pulled out a bottle of Tylenol and walked over to my liquor cabinet and took out a bottle of water. "Here." I handed the pills and water to her. "Take a moment, and then go to my bathroom. There's an extra toothbrush there you can have."

She nodded and popped the top to painkillers, took two pills, and then swallowed. "Thank you," she whispered.

"You're welcome. Now go clean up. I'll go through what you've found. And Ainsley?"

"Yeah?"

"You said you still might be able to stand for your friend. What time is the wedding today?"

"Two p.m."

I nodded. "Call your friends. I'll have my driver take you home and then take you to the wedding." I smirked at my next set of words. "I'll send along some of my best Scotch with you as well."

She groaned. "I am never touching Scotch again for the rest of my life." Ainsley turned toward the bathroom, and I chuckled in her wake. She paused by the door and turned to face me. "Thank you."

I looked up and met her gaze. "For what? I can't imagine why you'd be thanking me. From what I recall, you're furious at me. The words, 'that ship has fucking sailed'?"

She covered her face again. "I wish I could have destroyed that before you found it." She looked at me with a shrug. "The 'thanks' is for letting me go to the wedding. And sending something as a gift. I'm sure they'll appreciate it."

She pulled her phone from her pocket, dialed a number, and brought the phone to her ear as she closed the door behind her.

Walking into my office today, I hadn't expected to find the note from Ainsley—nor Ainsley, for that matter—but it had opened my eyes to something I hadn't realized before.

Ainsley was a woman with needs. She wanted me, and I never saw it. Hell, I never saw *her*. She'd called me out on that in her letter.

I was an asshole, and yet she still wanted me. Why? I thought women wanted the theoretical knight to rescue them from the theoretical tower where the theoretical dragon held them hostage.

Fuck… *Am I the dragon?*

With a groan, I folded the note and placed it in my desk drawer. I needed to focus on my case and getting Lance free. Ainsley and her fucking lust note would have to wait. I pulled my phone out and sent a text to my driver to have the limo ready in ten minutes.

I reviewed the notes she left for me and was happy to discover this new witness was nowhere to be seen during the party. Ainsley also had the social media giant, Facebook, open to our apparent witness's page.

Lo and behold, he was lip-locked with the accuser, Miss Miranda Cooper.

"Well, if that isn't a bunch of shit. How the hell did the prosecutor not get this information? Or were they just grasping at straws?"

Many times, lawyers tried to take down giants for the exposure. If this court-appointed attorney had gone up against my firm and won, it would have gotten him reputable points. However, looking like an ass clown would only sink his reputation even further.

Ainsley stepped out of the bathroom, and she appeared freshened. Her hair was smoothed back into a ponytail, the smeared makeup was washed away, and her face was no longer red with blush.

"Thank you for the toothbrush," she offered in a soft voice. "I appreciate it."

"No problem," I said and stood from my seat. "You did good finding all this information on our guy. I guess my problem now is, why did the prosecutor not discover this as well? Seems it was a waste of time, honestly."

She nodded and held her gaze to the floor. "May I get that ride now?"

She was like a dormouse inside a trap that was hell-bent on keeping her in the dark. Nowhere to go, nowhere to run, yet the door was just in front of her.

I took a step toward her and pushed my hands into my pockets. "Yes, you may go. Please send my apologies to the wedding party for keeping you. Were you able to get ahold of them?"

She nodded. "Yes, thanks."

"Great. Oh, before I forget." I sidestepped Ainsley and opened the liquor cabinet once more. I pulled out a bottle of Scotch and handed it to her. "My compliments to the happy couple. The limo will be waiting for you downstairs."

She nodded, accepted the gift, and then turned toward the door.

"Ainsley?"

She paused and looked over her shoulder. Her eyes were light blue like the sky on an early Sunday morning as the sun had just risen over the horizon. Her lips were slightly full with a soft pink tone. I suddenly felt the need to kiss her.

"We'll pick this up on Monday morning."

She held my gaze for a moment, and a blush rushed her neck and cheeks. She looked to the floor, and then with a curt nod, she closed the door behind her.

I walked over to my desk and leaned against the edge. I wasn't sure what to make of Ainsley Speire. Whether it was for a fun frolic or for something more, there was something here to be tested. I wasn't ready to settle down, but the honesty in Ainsley's hate note shifted something inside me, and damn it if I didn't want to explore that . . . and her.

Now that her cards were on the table, it was time for me to decide if I was up for the challenge or if I wanted to fold and walk away.

And I never walked away from a challenge.

CHAPTER FIVE

AINSLEY

Shit. Shit. Shit. Shit over fucking shit and more shit!

I couldn't believe what had happened. Chase's Scotch ... the letter ...

I am so fired.

Riding in the car on the way to my home was like a high-end walk of shame, just without the sex. Chase had walked in to find his booze in one of my hands and a scorching sexual note in the other. And on his mouth? His sexy lips were pulled into a Cheshire grin. It was a smile I had witnessed him give his latest arm candy. It was a knowing smile—one of a man on the hunt for his latest prey.

I opened my phone and looked over my missed calls, texts, and emails. Who sent emails anymore? Apparently my friends when they couldn't get ahold of me. Last night was the rehearsal dinner, and I'd missed it. No one should be surprised. This new career I'd opted for had taken up so much of my time. Between studies, my bar exam, and working in Chase's office, it was a wonder I still had any personal connections at all.

I ground my teeth and pressed the Call button to dial the bride-to-be and then held my breath as her phone rang.

"Where the hell are you?" Ashley answered.

"Hey, yeah, I'm safe. No worries about me."

"Dude, it's my fucking wedding day. No time for sarcasm." She sighed into the phone, and I felt like foul shit. "Listen, are you coming?"

"Yes," I told her in a lowered voice. "I was forced to work last night." I wanted to tell her all about drinking Chase's Scotch and my drunken note, but all in due time. Today was her day, not my day to spoil.

Keep your head on straight, Speire. She has enough on her hands to not have to worry about your horrible decision-making.

"We all figured as much, but hey, a nice note would have been helpful that you wouldn't make the dinner. Damn it, Mom!" she yelled. "Don't make me bleed! That was close!"

"Why would your mom make you bleed?" I asked, hoping to get the topic off me.

"She's trying to pin my dress. Apparently I lost too much weight! Who the hell loses too much weight, Ainsley?"

I laughed softly into the phone. I loved Ashley. We had been friends since high school when her family moved to Dallas. She joined one of the clubs I was a part of, and we had been inseparable ever since.

"How far away are you from the church?" Ashley asked, pulling me from my thoughts.

I hadn't paid much attention. I looked up to the red light we were at.

"We're driving down Elm Street and should be to you soon. I need to pick up a few things first, and then I'm there. I promise."

Ashley wanted to marry in the historic church in downtown Dallas. It was a large off-white cathedral, and many of the windows were stained glass. It was beautiful and completely suited her style.

When I decided to marry, I'd be happy with running off to Vegas and getting married by Elvis. My parents would never forgive me, but it would be my wedding, not theirs.

"Okay, we're in the back changing room. I have your dress here. I had hoped you'd show up today and not pick your fucking job over my damned wedding day."

"Ashley, I said I was sorry about last night. I promise I'll make up to you. And Chase sends his congratulations with a large bottle of Scotch."

"Good. I have cups here. Let's break it open to help soothe my nerves." She groaned into the phone. "Fucking wedding shoes. Get here, Ainsley. Bye."

She hung up before I had a chance to say anything back. I tucked my phone in my bag and leaned toward the driver. "I'll give you a large tip if you can get me there in five minutes."

The driver looked in the rearview mirror, his brown eyes staring back at me. "Miss, there's no need to tip. It's my pleasure. Hold tight. We'll be there soon."

With a sigh, I sat back in the seat and rested my head. Closing my eyes, I could only imagine what I'd look like walking in. Yesterday's makeup and clothes, hair not done... I was the worst friend ever. This was the part of my job I hated. I detested being away from everyone, but if I wanted this to work, I needed to put in the hours, the work, the blood, sweat, and tears. Because if I didn't, then what would be the point of it all?

I needed experience. The experience came with cases. Cases only came because they knew you won.

"All right, miss, we're here."

I lifted my head and checked the time on my phone. I was still early enough for me to shower and rush to the church and stand up for my friend. Dry shampoo and makeup will do wonders for anyone.

◆ ◆ ◆ ◆

Always the bridesmaid, never the bride.

What a way to chastise someone for not being the center of attention. It was a horrible statement to mutter to anyone, and of course, today, all the single ladies heard it from all the married ladies.

Why was this a thing?

I sat in a plastic chair with my legs crossed and sipped on my Moscato. The wedding had gone off perfectly. Ashley was beautiful, and her dress was the highlight of the occasion. Her new husband admitted to renting a tuxedo. I'll never understand the fuss of a wedding dress when the groom's attire seemed to be nothing but a joke.

Another bridesmaid I had never met sat at the table with me, nursing a glass of beer. The DJ blasted the *Wobble* song, and every person who knew the song—and also those who didn't—danced on the floor the best they could.

Our dresses were peach, sleeveless, and fitted down to our knees, where they flared out in tulle. I felt like we were going to our high school prom all over again.

It wasn't that I didn't like weddings. I didn't like that I felt very single . . . and had Chase on my mind. Across the room, a group of men were talking. Most had already removed their sports jackets and loosened their ties. A younger one with sandy-blond hair made eye contact with me and smiled.

I laughed under my breath and downed the rest of my Moscato. One of the waiters walked by, and I snagged a fresh glass from his tray. As I settled back into my seat, the sandy-blond guy started crossing the floor toward me.

Oh, I am so not in the mood for this.

"Would you like to dance?" he asked.

"No, thanks."

"'No thanks' you don't want to dance, or 'no thanks' you're not sure how? I'm happy to teach you."

I looked up at him and frowned. "What?"

"Come on, let's dance."

I shook my head. "No. Go away."

"Ahh, come—"

"The lady said no," the other bridesmaid said.

I glanced over to her and raised my glass. "Mazel tov."

She grinned and followed with, "Thank you."

"Now please go ask someone else," I said. "My feet hurt, I'm hungover, and I confessed to the lawyer I work for that I want to do awful things to him. So unless you have a get-out-of-jail-free card or a way to turn back time, step back and leave me alone."

His brows rose, and he took a few steps back in retreat. "Right, sorry I asked." He disappeared into the crowd of dancers.

I turned back to the table, grateful to be alone once more. I probably looked like a princess completely washed up after waiting for her knight in shining armor to arrive...but he never did.

"Fuck that," I said to myself.

"Fuck what?" the other bridesmaid asked.

I glanced up at her and shook my head. "Just musing over today's events."

"Something about doing awful things to your boss?"

I chuckled. "Yeah, that happened." I leaned onto my left arm and sipped my wine. "I missed rehearsal last night because of him."

She nodded. "We all heard about that. I'm Missy, Ashley's cousin."

"Ainsley," I said and reached across the table with my hand. She took it and gave it a shake. "Nice to meet you, Missy."

"Nice to meet you too."

A silence fell between us for a bit.

"Are you here alone?"

She nodded. "Yep, sure am. Seems you are as well?"

"Yes, ma'am." I looked over to the dancefloor. Ashley and her new husband, Brad, took to the song they had picked out for their wedding dance. "I'm really happy for her, but I'm in no rush to find Mr. Right."

"But if Mr. Right Now were to approach?" Missy asked.

I looked at her and laughed. I liked her. "Yeah, Mr. Right Now has been fun in the past."

"So, what're your plans come Monday?"

I frowned and lifted a brow. "What do you mean?"

"When you have to go back to work with that lawyer. Are you going to walk in like a baller, or will you walk in and not make eye contact?"

I shrugged. "I haven't quite figured that out yet. I'm more of a dragon kind of girl. I don't need a man to rescue me from a tower. I'll tame the dragon and ride the beast out of the kingdom."

She laughed and pointed to me. "I love that! That shit needs to be on a shirt!"

"Well, Missy, damn it, make it happen!"

"So," she asked and leaned over. "Do you plan to line up for the bouquet?"

I laughed and shook my head. "Hell, no. You?"

She shrugged. "If it's an opportunity to push someone aside who is desperate enough to grab for it? Then yes, yes I'll play."

I shook my head. "You play dirty."

She winked. "Yes, but it's better than not playing at all."

"Maybe, but I don't need the bouquet."

"No, but you can take a flower from it," said another voice.

I glanced up to find Ashley standing in front of me. She pulled a peach rose from her bouquet and handed it to me. "I decided to say fuck tradition and do my own thing. So instead of having people push each other out of the way"—Ashley glared at Missy—"I thought it would be fun to give everyone a rose from my arrangement instead and send them off with well-wishes for the future."

I brought the rose close and inhaled the familiar fragrance. I noticed the center of it was a dark peach, almost pink. The outer edges of the flower were almost white.

"The roses are beautiful," I told her. "So are you."

She smiled. "Thank you. Now, if I may be so bold to ask, will you dance with me?"

I grinned and stood. "Well hell, I can't turn down the bride."

"Exactly. Let's go!"

We made it to the dancefloor just as the DJ was starting one of our high school dance songs. The Spice Girls' "Wannabe" started, and I couldn't help laughing. Ashley took my hand and pulled me to the center of the floor.

I laughed and held my hands in the air while I danced with my friend who had long since forgiven me for not showing up to her rehearsal last night.

Across the room stood a man in the shadows. He wore a tuxedo, and his hair was styled back. I couldn't quite see who he was for the darkness that fell over his features, but even from here, he had the build of a familiar man. When a camera flashed, my breath stilled in my chest.

"Chase?" I whispered and looked toward the darkened corner of the room. The man moved toward the light, and I realized then it wasn't him. I closed my eyes and flinched when my arm was grabbed. I looked to see Ashley holding on to me.

"When I get back from our honeymoon, we'll talk about what happened. Is that okay?"

I smiled and pulled her into my arms. "Oh, woman. You're always doing everything for me. No, it's okay. Don't worry about me. I'll be fine. You go on and have your honeymoon and start making babies. I'll see you when you get back." I let her go and stepped back.

I nodded and turned when her new husband took her by the hand. I headed back toward the table I was sitting at with Missy, the other bridesmaid, and decided it would be a good time to make a break for it. I needed air, I was tired, and I wanted to sleep through the rest of this weekend.

When Monday arrived, I had no idea what I would be walking into.

CHAPTER SIX

CHASE

I wasn't sure how many times I had read Ainsley's love/hate note over the weekend, but the folds of the paper began to tear. Darkened spots that marked the page where Scotch had splashed when she'd written the letter became something of a road map. My fingers traced over the parchment, and the indentions of her scribe reminded me these were her words that were indeed on the paper.

Not many called me out on bullshit, but Ainsley had. I wasn't sure how I felt about that, but it had opened my eyes to something I hadn't realized before. Ainsley was a beautiful woman. She was a few years younger than me, but she held herself in high regard and never let her emotions show.

Well, at least until Saturday morning, when I walked in on her hungover and passed out on my desk. She'd had fear in her eyes when she woke to me holding the letter she'd written. I was positive she'd never had any intention of me finding it, yet here we were.

Ainsley wasn't the type I normally would go after. Maybe what I chased was only for sport. Get them in my bed, fuck them, and then show them to the door. Sex was no more than two people enjoying the benefits of an orgasm and the occasional blow job. I never even kissed anyone. That was too intimate by my standards. The last woman I kissed was my ex, but that was before I walked in on her fucking my former best friend.

I liked tall, slender women with long hair and full breasts, full asses. I preferred blondes over brunettes and redheads. And I had no time in my life for a relationship or children. My life was about me, and it had been that way for a long time. I had been called shallow more than once. It had never bothered me in the past. If the words came from Ainsley, however, I was pretty sure it would make me cringe.

Now I found myself wanting to see Ainsley walk through the office door, briefcase in hand. I wanted to see her in her office attire of a knee-length skirt, blouse, and heels. Her hair was auburn and her eyes this sea of green I felt I could get lost in. Her body was fit but not the slender build I normally went after. Ainsley had curves in all the right places. She had this hourglass figure that up until Saturday morning, I never noticed. Now I wanted to hold her naked in my arms and devour every curve.

Why? Why now?

Because she'd told me off.

Because she wanted me, needed me, and longed for me to notice her. And I was the asshole who never did.

Her tits were stacked, her ass was round and perfect, and her legs were just long enough to wrap around my waist. I also wanted them wrapped around my neck while I tasted and licked her, ass to clit.

My dick throbbed, and I needed some relief. I wanted to lay Ainsley in my bed and fuck her. Maybe doing so would get her out of my head. She would be a conquest of sorts. Maybe it was the age-old "wanting something you can't have" mentality.

Whatever it was, I wanted it. I wanted *her*.

But now . . . she resented me for never noticing her. That could be hard to come back from but not impossible. I loved a good challenge, and Ainsley was next.

I looked up at the clock in my office—five minutes to eight. Ainsley normally would have been here by now. Would she come back after what had happened Saturday morning? Would she brave her nerves and face me? Hell, would I face her?

The door to my firm opened, and I glanced down the hall to see Ainsley walking through it. For a moment, she was a goddess of sex appeal, and hell if I didn't want to confess my sins.

"Good morning," she said to the receptionist with a smile.

Ainsley wore a white button-down blouse with a thin black ribbon tied into a bow under the folded lace collar. She had on a calf-length pencil skirt that was fitted to her body and heels that lifted her by a few inches.

My mouth watered, and I wanted to devour the woman there on the spot.

Her long locks of curled hair were pulled to one side and tumbled over her shoulder. Her lips were painted with a light-red gloss, and every part of me wanted to see them around the head of my cock.

"Fuck," I groaned and rubbed a hand over the erection inside my pants. How did this woman suddenly have such control over me, when I never saw it prior to now?

You want what you can't have.

Ainsley crossed the reception area, her heels striking the tile with each step. Her steps seemed to grow slower, and she stared at the floor and hugged her arms around her chest.

Was she upset? Nervous? Scared?

"Good morning, Ainsley," I said before I realized I'd even muttered the words.

She raised her eyes and met mine, and her endless sea of green captured me. God, did I want her.

She stepped into my office and stood in the entry. "Good morning, Mr. Newstrom."

"Close the door, please," I asked.

As she did, her body seemed timid. Like a rabbit was being stalked by a fox and said fox just invited her into his den. The door clicked closed, and Ainsley slowly turned back to face me. Her eyes were once again focused on the floor.

"What can I help you with this morning, Mr. Newstrom?"

She was scared, and rightfully so. She'd told the owner of the firm she was working for in hopes of landing a position once her bar results came in to, more or less, fuck off.

"I wanted to thank you for the evidence you found to support our client."

She nodded. "It was nothing."

"Ainsley," I said and stood from my seat. "Please, come sit down. I think we need to have a talk."

She closed her eyes, and her throat moved as she swallowed. She nodded and approached one of the chairs across my desk. The perfume she wore filled the air with a light floral fragrance. It wasn't too heavy and was perfect for her. She sat down and set her briefcase on the floor next to herself. Ainsley then crossed one leg over the other, her skirt just short enough that I could barely see the underside of her thigh.

I imagined my hand running up the outside of her leg while I settled between her thighs, ready to claim her as mine.

"Yes, Mr. Newstrom?" she asked, breaking my thoughts.

With a sigh, I crossed to the front of my desk and leaned against the edge of it. "Saturday morning, when I came into the office—"

"Yes, I'm so sorry," she blurted out and cut me off. "I don't know what I was thinking, and honestly, it never should have happened."

I raised my brows. She still refused to meet my gaze.

"Is that how you really feel?"

She lifted her gaze and met mine. "I'm sorry? What do you mean?"

"Are you really sorry you wrote that letter to me?"

She tried to meet my gaze, but her eyes darted back and forth as if she wasn't sure which eye to focus on.

I pulled my lips into a smirk and lifted a brow. "To say it surprised me would be an understatement."

She nodded, blinked, and then looked to my chest, back to my eyes, and then to the floor once more. "If you don't mind," she started, "can we forget it ever happened?"

A blush crept up her neck to her ears and then her cheeks. I wanted to watch her squirm in her seat. I cleared my throat to give her my thoughts on the subject. No, I didn't want to forget it. I wanted to explore our options and see where we ended up. I wanted to take her right here on my desk. I wanted to grip her ass as tight as I could while I fucked her from behind.

Instead, she squared her shoulders and sat up straight in her chair. "I have work to do, sir, so if you don't mind . . . " She began to stand, when the intercom buzzed.

"Mr. Newstrom," the receptionist called, "you have a

visitor. And I'm sorry, sir, she insisted on seeing you."

As she finished her sentence, my door opened. On the other side was my ex, Patricia. The woman was long and lean, her bottle-blond hair pulled into a ponytail. She had bright-blue eyes, was tan by way of spray tanning, and was the vainest person I'd ever met . . . aside from myself.

She smirked and stepped inside. She waved off Ainsley as if she weren't in the room.

"Chase, darling," she began. "There's a fundraiser in a few weeks, and your firm has donated quite a bit of money for the cause. It's a black-tie social event, and we must go together."

I raised my brows. Who the fuck did Patricia think she was talking to?

"Of course I know about the event. My firm puts it on, so yes, I'm aware." I glanced at Ainsley and found a small grin tugging at her lips. "Furthermore, I'm already going with someone else. Now, unless you have anything related to the case I'm working on, Ainsley and I are quite busy this morning. We have a court appearance to prepare for."

Patricia glanced down to Ainsley and sneered in disgust. That told me everything I needed to know about Patricia . . . as well as myself. For the first time, I saw myself through someone else's eyes, and to be quite honest, it was extremely disappointing.

"So what are you saying?" she asked.

"We have court," Ainsley repeated and stood from her chair. "Mr. Newstrom, I'll grab everything we need for today. I'll see about scheduling a celebratory party for our defendant, if you'd like?"

I nodded. "Sounds perfect. I appreciate that, and I know our guy will too."

"Who are you defending?" Patricia asked.

"Well, if you were actually interested, you should turn on the news," Ainsley told her as she turned and walked out my office door.

"Well, she's just a little bitch, isn't she?" Patricia said.

I smiled. I couldn't help myself. "No, she's a promising up-and-coming future attorney who just took the bar. She has a bright future ahead of her. Now, if you don't mind, I have work to do. I'm sure you'll find a date for the event. Or go stag. No difference to me, Patricia."

I stepped past her and held my door open. Looking at the woman now, I didn't know what I ever saw in her. It was crazy I once thought she could've been the love of my life.

At least until I'd caught her fucking my former best friend Mitch.

Patricia huffed and walked past me as she left. "You'll regret not taking me, Chase," she warned. "You know I have the connections to make you big."

"Amy," I called to our receptionist. "Please make sure Patricia leaves and that the door closes on her way out."

"Yes, sir," Amy called back.

"Fuck you, Chase," Patricia growled.

I smirked and shook my head. "That ship has fucking sailed." I closed the door to my office and the words *that ship has fucking sailed* haunted my mind. They were the same words that Ainsley had written in her letter.

With a sigh, I crossed my office, picked up my briefcase, and put inside everything we needed to get this case dropped. Soon, Lance Vanderbilt would be exonerated. The question, though, was what would become of Miranda Cooper? Lance's family could countersue, but would he agree to it? He was a nice kid, but his family was wealthy, and everything rode on their name and image.

I looked at the clock. We had an hour before the court session began. I walked toward my office door and reached for the handle just as the door opened. Ainsley stood before me.

Our eyes met, and for a brief moment, we were both motionless, speechless. There was a longing in her eyes that passed between us, and then it was gone.

"We should go," she said.

I nodded and held up my briefcase. "Lance should be a free man before the day's end."

"Then let's go get this done."

CHAPTER SEVEN

AINSLEY

"Not guilty," declared the jury foreman.

The new witness's testimony had been thrown out, and Lance was now a free man. His name and standing would require some massive cleanup, but we already had a PR firm working on just that.

Lance shook Chase's hand and then turned to me. "You both are amazing. Thank you so much."

"It was all Mr. Newstrom," I told him. And it was. He was the attorney. I was basically his errand girl.

Miranda Cooper's parents screamed out something about injustice as their daughter, in tears, kept saying, "I'm sorry," to Lance.

There was sadness in his eyes. He was happy to be free, but the cost was the friendship he had with this girl.

It was unfortunate she'd gone after his family's money. Greed was a nasty sin. As was lust. I looked over to Chase and found him watching me. My stomach fluttered with butterflies. I smiled and looked away.

I needed air. It felt like the courtroom was closing in the closer I stood next to Chase. I glanced at him again, and he was closing the distance to me. Shit. Double shit. *What am I supposed to do now?*

"Well done, Speire. I couldn't have done this without you."

I smiled and offered a slight shrug. "Yes, you would have. It just may have taken you longer."

He chuckled. "Listen, now that this is done, I'd like to ask—"

My phone rang, and it jolted me where I stood. I didn't know if Chase was about to ask me out or ask me if I had received my bar results. I didn't know what I would say if he asked me to grab a drink. It wouldn't be Scotch, that much I knew.

But why would he ever ask me on a date? He was so far out of my league. In my dreams and home with my trusty BOB were the only places I could imagine myself with Chase and not have to worry about rejection.

"I'm sorry. Hang on," I said and fished my phone out. It was my sister. "Hey," I answered. "I'm in court." Well, sort of. The case was over, but she didn't need to know that.

"Obviously not or you wouldn't have answered. I watched enough *Law and Order* to know that much."

I laughed into the phone. She was a stylist in downtown Fort Worth and loved what she did. She was a sort of therapist for the majority of her clients.

"Well, you got me there. But listen, let me call you back. We just won and need to pack up."

"Oh, did the rapist get off?" she asked.

"That's not very nice. He was set up."

"Sure, whatever. Call me when you get time. We'll go have a drink to celebrate your win."

"Love you. Goodbye." I hung up without giving her the opportunity to say anything further.

"Who was that?" Chase asked.

"My sister. Well, congratulations today on your win. You deserved it. Unless there's anything else, I need to run. Leave whatever needs to be completed on my desk, and I'll have it done ASAP."

He nodded. "Very well. Enjoy your afternoon."

I met his gaze once more. I didn't want him to ask me whatever he had planned, so I hurried out of the courtroom before he changed his mind and I combusted from overheating with lust.

I pulled up to my sister's shop in Fort Worth. The day was still young, and the atmosphere was busy with women getting their hair washed, cut, and colored. In the back sat pedicure massage chairs, and behind that was the massage parlor and facial rooms. My sister did it all and made pretty good money at it. She loved what she did and had tried many times to get me to go into business with her.

"I'm not one to have enough patience to work with hair or listen to why so-and-so's husband won't have sex with her," I'd told her many times.

"It's not all about that," she had countered. "It's fun and you get to make great . . . and interesting friends."

Eight years later, I was out of school and waiting to hear if I'd passed the bar.

"Ainsley!" my sister, Everly, called as I opened the door to her shop. She was a complete extrovert. Everly could talk to almost anyone anywhere. She never knew an enemy.

Her hair was shoulder-length and blond with caramel

lowlights. She loved wearing dark-red lipstick. Today's outfit consisted of a halter top, denim capris, and ballet flats. She wore a black smock to protect her clothes. The front of it was lined with hair clips, her sheers and clippers, and a dust brush.

"Hey, sis," I said as I stepped inside.

She stopped what she was doing long enough to meet me halfway for a hug. "What brings you by?"

With a sigh, I lowered my eyes to the floor. "I think I fucked up," I whispered.

She tilted my head up and looked into my eyes. Her green eyes had specks of gold and looked just like our mother's. "Did you fuck your boss?"

I shook my head. "Not yet."

"Oh, hell," she whispered and laid her hands on my shoulders. "Let me finish up Mrs. Gilbert, and I'll clear my schedule for the rest of today." She turned to the receptionist and grabbed her book. "I need you to mark me out after my current appointment. Family emergency."

The receptionist nodded and punched a few keys into the computer and then picked up the phone to start making the necessary calls.

"Are you all right?" she asked.

I nodded. "Go finish up. I'll wait for you."

She touched my cheek and then pointed toward the back wall. "Room three is empty. Go wait in there. The room is dark and is relaxing. There are essential oils in there to help in meditation."

"Okay," I told her and made my way to the back. The smell of hair color and hairspray faded as I walked into the back massage area.

Room three, as she directed, was indeed empty. I closed

the door behind me. On the wall just inside was my sister's license to perform esthetician work, with an image of her. She was beautiful and had an infectious smile.

With a sigh, I walked over to the massage table and ran my hand over the top. It was soft and warm. Curious, I lifted the blanket and found a heating pad turned on at the ready. Not wanting to waste this opportunity, I set my purse down, removed my shoes, and climbed onto the table. I lay down on my back, laid my head on the bed pillow, and closed my eyes.

The heat was welcoming, and the smell of eucalyptus was nice. Images of Chase drifted through my mind. From his business suit to his workout clothes, the man was sexy as sin. My mind went to a dream I often had of Chase . . .

He slid his hands down my sides, and his lips captured mine. He was soft like velvet and tasted like the juiciest plum. I wanted to devour him.

He tilted my head up and pulled my body firm against his. He slipped a hand behind my head and tangled it in my hair. Giving my hair a firm tug, he yanked my head to the side and nibbled up and down my neck.

I gasped and slid my fingers under my skirt and panties. Pressing my fingers against my clit, I moved them side to side, my mind telling me it was Chase who had his fingers inside me.

"I need you," I whispered.

"Let me fuck you," he teased back.

A sudden knock on the door brought me from my daydream with a gasp. I quickly pulled my fingers from my sex, straightened myself, and sat up.

"Hey, sis, you in here?" Everly asked and peeked inside.

"You said room three," I told her and prayed the blush on

my cheeks wouldn't give away what I was just doing.

She stepped inside, and I hoped she couldn't hear my heart beating five hundred miles an hour.

"Okay, so let's talk." She locked the door and climbed onto the table next to me. "Spill. What happened?"

I gripped the table I was sitting on and closed my eyes. I told her about almost missing Ashley's wedding, drinking a fuck ton of Chase's Scotch, and writing the letter.

"Okay, so you wrote a nastygram. No harm no foul. Right?"

I opened my eyes and looked at her. My brows were pressed together with a plea for her to read my mind without me saying as much. I bit my lip and felt my eyes burn with the threat of tears.

"Oh, shit," she whispered. "How did he get the letter?"

"I passed out on his desk. I woke up Saturday morning, and he was standing over me."

"Oh, shit," she repeated. "Okay, so tell me this. Was he frowning or smiling?"

"More smiling than frowning."

"What do you mean?" she asked.

I looked to my hands and twisted my fingers together. "He had this sly smile, like a Cheshire grin."

"Oh, hell," she squealed. "You realize he wants you as much as you want him?"

I frowned and met her gaze. "And you've officially sniffed too much hair product."

"Oh, my God, sis. Do you not see what is right in front of you? If he was smiling, smirking, whatever, if he looked like he wanted to eat you alive, this is a good thing!"

I bit my lip once more. "Really?" I whispered. I had a hard

time believing this, but he *had* smiled.

"Yes," she insisted. "And as your sister, I encourage you to go for it."

"Go for what?" I asked. "I'm so not his type."

"What is his type, then?"

I sighed and shrugged. "Tall and thin. Model perfect, hasn't eaten for days, and hangs on every word he says as if they're absolutely interested."

"And they have no idea what he's talking about, am I right?"

I nodded. "Exactly."

"Well, you will know what he's talking about when you converse, and there's a chance you are his type but he didn't realize it until you pointed it out to him."

"I pointed nothing out other than I'm a damned fool who should have never touched his Scotch. Said letter would never be in existence."

"You're a pussy," she stated.

I frowned. "Excuse me?"

"You're a fucking pussy, sis. Tall, dark, and gorgeous wants you, and you're too scared to pounce on him like the sexy feline you are."

I laughed at her explanation. "Number one, I'm not a fucking cat. And two, I'll never pounce on him."

"Why the fuck not?" she asked. "What's stopping you?"

"Well, the simple fact that I'm working at his law firm and he could throw me away in disgust."

She groaned and hopped down from the table. "Do me a favor and fucking go for it, okay? Please, do us both the favor. Hook up with him, get married, and have children so Mom will quit asking me when I'm getting married and having babies."

I laughed and hopped down from the table. I pulled Everly into a hug. "Well, you are older."

"And I rather like my single life, thank you very much," she told me. "I'm not ready to settle down."

"I'm not either."

She smiled and cupped my cheeks. "You may not have a choice once you go for Chase Newstrom. He may sweep you off your feet."

"That's what I'm afraid of," I told her. "Falling for the man and him breaking my heart."

"But you won't know that until you take the leap. Now stop being a scaredy-cat and show him what kind of panther on the prowl you are."

I shook my head. "I'm not a cat."

"Then prove to me you're not a pussy, Ainsley. Man up and pounce him hard!"

"You're relentless!"

"And you love me! Come on, I'm off the rest of the day. Let's go shopping and find you something sexy to wear into the office tomorrow."

With a sigh, I nodded in agreement. I did enjoy shopping, and hanging with my sister always put me in a better mood.

Tomorrow would be here soon enough. And if Everly had her way, she'd dress me up in something way too sexy for the office . . . and a part of me wanted her to do just that.

CHAPTER EIGHT

CHASE

The very next day after we won the case for Lance Vanderbilt, our PR firm was already hard at work at clearing his name. Some firms frowned upon us, as we represented defendants, but if the person was innocent, I considered it an honorable challenge to prove it.

I lived for the adrenaline that pumped through my veins when I heard "not guilty."

I haven't lost a case yet, but I also didn't represent people who weren't innocent. And what many failed to realize was that I had resources at my disposal to help victims of crimes. I might not have represented them, but I also didn't want to see them suffer.

Ainsley hadn't been to the office—that I could see anyway—since I won the case. I wasn't sure if she was avoiding me or if she was following up on other things. I hoped it was the latter. I wanted to see her, talk to her, devour every inch of her.

I crossed my office to pour another cup of coffee, when I heard the front door open.

"Good morning, Ainsley," Amy, our receptionist, called.

"Good morning. How are you?" Ainsley returned.

"Fine, and you?"

"I'm good, thank you."

"Hey, new outfit?" I heard Amy ask.

"Yes, thanks for noticing. It's not too much, though?"

Now curious, I peeked out my door and could only see Amy's backside.

"Not at all. It's beautiful. I wish I were bold enough to wear red like that. You look stunning!"

"Well, thank you, then." Ainsley's heels struck the tile as she made her way down the hallway. I leaned against the counter next to my coffeemaker and sipped my liquid gold, and I almost choked on the hot substance when she passed by.

Ainsley had on candy-apple red pants, a black satin top, and a matching red dress jacket. She wore black and red heels that complemented the outfit and carried a black purse. Her hair was pulled to the nape of her neck in a twisted bun with red and black pearl pins holding it in place. She looked like she'd just stepped off a runway.

She glanced over to me through the entryway, and it was as if time slowed. Her red lips pulled into a smile as she passed and continued down the hall.

Instantly I grew hard. What the hell was this woman doing to me? How did I not notice her, her body, her tits, her ass, her lips, her legs...her...before now? Once she was out of sight, I reached down with my free hand and adjusted my growing erection.

Last night, I'd opened a bottle of Scotch and had a few drinks while I reread her letter...again. I'd imagined she was there with me, stroking my cock as she sat on her knees. It wasn't often I masturbated to thoughts of a woman, but last night I had. Once at my desk and again in the shower.

In the shower, I would have pressed her hands to the tile

and pulled her hair back while I took her from behind. Her perfect ass slapping against my pelvis while we fucked with hot water streaming over our bodies.

"Mr. Newstrom?"

Speak of the devil as her voice filled the silence of my office. I looked up to Ainsley standing in my doorway with her red and black outfit. I smiled, and it took every ounce of power I had to hold her gaze. I wanted to run the length of her body with my eyes, imagine her naked, legs around my face and then my waist.

"Yes?" I asked through a crack in my voice. I cleared my throat and tried again. "Yes, Ainsley?"

"All the documentation has been completed and turned into the court."

"Very good."

"Will there be anything else I can do for you today?"

Whoa...

Yes, there's so much you can do. Come drop to your knees and let me fuck your mouth. Then lie on my desk so I can fuck you the way you need to be fucked.

"No, that will be all for now."

She nodded and began to turn away.

"Ainsley?"

She lifted her brows and looked at me. "Yes?"

"You did really well on this case. You're going to make an amazing attorney."

She smiled, and it was genuine. "Thank you, sir."

"Please, call me Chase?"

She nodded and crossed her hands in front of her body. "Thank you, Chase."

Hearing my name on her lips caused my dick to twitch again.

Down boy.

"Can I ask you a question?" I started.

She nodded again. "Of course."

"Step into my office first."

Ainsley hesitated for a moment and then stepped inside.

I moved around her and closed the door behind her. She met my gaze. She absolutely took my breath away.

"Since we won this case," I started and put some space between us, "I'd like to take you for a celebratory drink."

Her face flushed, and she looked to the floor. She crossed her arms over her body and hugged herself. Ainsley bit her lip and then met my gaze.

She was so beautiful. There was a beauty about her I don't think she realized she had. Still, I could kick myself for not seeing it before now. I took a hesitant step toward her, and Ainsley blinked and slightly backstepped.

"A drink?" she asked.

I nodded and took another step closer. "The Vanderbilts won, and we should celebrate." Although I rarely did this for other cases, this one was different. And this wasn't about the case but about getting Ainsley out from the office in a more private setting.

"Is that such a good idea?" she asked in a small, soft voice, her eyes never leaving mine. Fear did not appear in her eyes, but longing . . . maybe desperation . . . did. She raised her brows and parted her lips. I could see the crest of her teeth, and then her tongue quickly darted out and licked her upper lip.

"I'd like to think so," I offered. As much as I wanted to press her to the wall and kiss her, I decided to keep some space between us. It was better for her since we were still in my office. The last thing I ever wanted was to ruin Ainsley's reputation before her career even started or for her to feel pressured into anything with me.

I could smell her floral perfume, so light yet so intoxicating. It had become something I wanted to smell every day.

"Chase," she whispered. "About the letter—"

"Don't," I cut her off. "I want to thank you for what you did." Double entendre—thank her for her help on the case and thank her for opening my eyes to seeing her for the first time. There was also a hint of rejection. I could see it, feel it. I didn't handle it well, but with Ainsley, I could be a patient man.

Finally, she offered a nod. "Okay. I'll have a drink with you."

I smiled, and the weight of rejection lifted. "Great!" I sounded almost a little too excited. "How about tonight, after we're done for the day?"

"That soon?" she asked.

"Why not?" I took a small step closer to her. I couldn't help myself. My eyes drifted to her breasts. They were held perfectly in the bra she wore, the top of her mounds peeking out just over the top of her blouse. Her waist was slender but curvy. Her hips were a little wide but perfect in her hourglass shape. And her legs ended in those sexy-as-hell-shoes. I looked into her eyes once more. "I'd be honored if you joined me."

She cleared her throat, and her breath huffed in delectation. She pursed her lips together, the red rouge rubbing together in earnest. "Okay," she whispered.

Before I realized what I was doing, I drew my fingers over the edge of her cheekbone down to her jawline. I dropped my hand and turned away from her.

"I'm . . . I didn't mean to touch you." I met her gaze once more, and my hazed craziness evaporated at her smile. "I'll send you the time and place."

She looked to the ground. As I turned my back to circle my desk, she cleared her throat.

"Will there be anything else?" she asked.

I needed to let go of the desperation of wanting to touch her, the need of *I want to fuck you on my desk right goddamned now.*

"No, we're done here. Thank you for your time." I picked up some papers and faked interest in what I was reading.

"Very well," she said, and I heard my door open.

I glanced over my shoulder and watched Ainsley disappear on the other side as it closed. I let a long breath go. Every bit of my being had wanted to press her against the wall and kiss her, but I knew I shouldn't. I put the papers down and rubbed my face a few times.

I picked up my cell, pulled up the bar a few blocks from my office, and called to make a reservation. If we were going to do this, it had to be perfect—not just something that was thrown together last minute.

I glanced down and looked at the erection pressing against my dress pants. I wanted to go to my private bathroom and relieve myself, but a sadistic part of me wanted to see what tonight brought.

And I could not wait.

CHAPTER NINE

AINSLEY

I've never been more nervous about a date in my life. The ones I had been on before were easy. I knew what to expect.

Man meets woman.

Woman likes man.

Man asks woman out.

Woman accepts.

First date over dinner and maybe a movie.

Is there chemistry? No—you say thanks and move on. Yes—a second and third date.

Is the chemistry still there? No—say your thanks and again, move on. Yes—do you want to have sex? The answer should be yes, but if it isn't, move the hell on. However, if the sex is out-of-this-world spectacular, then agree to continue going out. If the sex is nothing short of awful, say your goodbye, and if required, change your phone number.

Normally I didn't get past the first or second date. Call me picky, but if I was going to spend time with someone, they needed to be worth it. I would expect their opinion to be the same.

As I looked myself over in the mirror, my stomach flipped a number of times at the prospect of sitting across from Chase tonight. It was no secret that he slept around. He'd never been known to have a girlfriend. So why was I so interested in this date?

Because he was hot as hell, and if rumors from his past conquests were true, he was amazing in the sack.

Why not have a good time?

"Because it's my career," I mumbled to myself. With a sigh, I ran my hands down my black cocktail dress. It was sleeveless and fitted down my body. It definitely showed off my curves, which I absolutely loved. The hem reached just above my knees. I'd paired the outfit with my black sling-back peep-toe heels. An encrusted butterfly sat on the side of each shoe. They were beautiful and one of my favorite pairs to wear.

I pulled my hair to the side and wrapped it into a bun. I pulled a few loose strands around my face and then set it with spray. The top of my dress was high cut, and the back crisscrossed with wide straps from the shoulders to my hips. The necklace I'd picked out had a silver chain with a black rose pendant outlined with small diamonds around the petals. I had earrings that matched as well.

I took a few steps back and inspected my outfit and accessories with satisfaction. I sighed and glanced down my body. I'd shaved earlier today, but it wasn't like I was going to drop my panties after dinner for a quick romp in his limo.

But if he seduced me and his hands were on my body . . . well, one might be willing to change their mind.

With a shiver, I picked up my black and silver clutch and headed back to my kitchen. My phone was lit, and when I picked it up, I saw I had a missed text from Chase.

I can't wait to see you.

*I'm waiting for the driver to get here. I'm
looking forward to seeing you as well.*

I stared at my text for a moment. With a groan, I pressed Send and waited. Why was I playing this silly cat-and-mouse game with the man who held my career in the palm of his hands? Why had I written that stupid letter? Why did he have to find it?

My phone chimed.

See you soon, then.

I put my phone inside my clutch when a knock at my door sounded. I walked across the room and peeked out the peephole to see Chase's driver, Andrew, standing there.

With a smile, I opened the door.

"Good evening, Miss Speire," Andrew said.

"Good evening, Andrew."

The man was older, with a thin build and bald. He smiled and motioned for me to join him.

"Shall we?" he asked.

"We shall," I returned and closed the door behind me and then locked it. "Thank you for picking me up tonight."

"It's never a problem."

Moments later, we pulled up to the Tipsy Alchemist, a bar in downtown Dallas. I had heard about this place and had wanted to come here for some time. Excitement to experience this place, with Chase's company, made tonight not feel so awkward.

Andrew pulled up to the valet parking area. One of the attendants opened my door and offered his hand. I took it and stepped out of the vehicle. I turned back to Andrew.

"Thank you again."

"You're more than welcome, Miss Speire."

The attendant closed the door and walked me to the maître d'. The man behind the podium looked up with a smile.

"Good evening. Do you have a reservation with us tonight?"

I nodded. "Yes, under Chase Newstrom." Saying his name fluttered the butterflies in my belly, and it brought a smile to my lips.

The maître d's eyes widened slightly, and he nodded. "Yes, madam, right this way." He snapped his fingers, and another attendant quickly made his way over to us. "Please escort Miss Speire to the private dining area where Mr. Newstrom awaits."

"I didn't give you my name," I told him in a soft voice.

He smiled. "Mr. Newstrom alerted us of your arrival, madam. We are here and ready to serve your every need tonight."

My brows rose. "Wow, well, okay, then." I wasn't quite sure what to think of this type of treatment. I was lucky to get my order correct the first time at McDonald's or even somewhere fancier, like Chili's. However, tonight, these were drinks and dinner I knew I couldn't afford.

Water would be on my bill tonight. Assuming, of course, they didn't charge for tap.

I was led inside, and the bar ambiance was soft and the lights dim. The temperature was on the chilly side. Upon entry, a large planter of cactus greens greeted us. Behind it was an open atmosphere of tables filled with people talking and drinking. On the far side of the room was the bar. It was filled with all sorts of alcohol, and the shelving looked like it was made of iron pipes. Each tabletop had a different arrangement, from pressure gauges to candelabra that had a steampunk feel to them.

"This way, Miss Speire," the attendant said.

As I followed him through the bar, I noticed there were corners blocked off with red velvet ropes. Small, quaint tables were inside the roped-off areas, with two chairs on either side of the table and a love seat along the wall.

"Wow," I whispered.

"Here we are," the attendant said as we came to a stop. We stood before a roped-off area that had closed red velvet curtains. He pulled one of the curtains to the side, and sitting on the love seat was Chase Newstrom.

He stood immediately. His dark-brown hair had been styled, and he wore a black suit and tie. He sipped his drink and set the glass down. Taking a few steps to where I stood, he smiled. His beautiful white teeth, kissable lips, and his eyes— his gorgeous, full-of-life blue eyes—stared directly into mine.

I was so fucked.

"Ainsley," Chase said and offered me his hand.

I accepted it, and the velvet rope was opened for me to pass through and then closed off again. The curtain was also pulled back into place, blocking us from the crowd of people just feet from where we stood.

His cologne invaded my nose, and I wanted to close my eyes and inhale, memorize his scent. I knew tonight would only last so long, and if we never did this again, I wanted to remember this for as long as I could.

"Are you all right?" he asked.

I opened my eyes and met his stare. I nodded. "Yes, and

if we're going to be honest with each other tonight, I'm a little nervous."

He chuckled and led me toward the love seat. "There's nothing to be nervous about."

I blinked, and then a laugh burst from me. "You're kidding, right? You're *the* Chase Newstrom. You barely gave me a second glance before . . . well . . . just before. Yet now we're here having drinks at a high-class establishment I could not afford even on my best day. So yes, I'm a little nervous."

He grinned. "I worked very hard to get where I am today. I see the same persistence and perseverance in you. You're going to make an incredible attorney, Ainsley."

I smiled and lowered my gaze to the table. "Thank you," I told him and meant it. With a sigh, I looked at him again. "Can we talk about that letter?"

He picked up his glass and took a sip. "What are you drinking tonight?"

"You can't answer a question with a question."

"Well, I can. And I did." He chuckled. "Now seriously, what are you drinking?"

"Dirty martini, extra olives."

He repeated my drink request to the bartender and then turned back to me. "So that letter."

My stomach flipped again, and my heart sped up. I nodded. "Yes. Look, I was drunk. I'm so sorry."

"Drunk on my Scotch," he added.

I felt my face heat up from blushing, and I nodded. "Yes, your Scotch. I'll replace it soon."

"Don't even worry about that," he said and turned toward me on the chaise. "I didn't realize you felt the way you did."

Now I knew my face was red because it was burning hot.

I wanted to look away, get up and run, but I couldn't. I needed to face this, talk to him about why I wrote what I did . . . and maybe get us past it.

"You're a beautiful man, Chase," I told him. "I see the women who swoon over you. It's hard to not be intimidated by your presence."

His brow rose. "Are you intimidated now?"

I shrugged my shoulder slightly. "Maybe?"

He chuckled. "Let me tell you my story, Ainsley. There's more to me than this pretty face and the women you say swoon over me."

I smiled and appreciated this moment. He wanted to let me in—at least on a part of himself, anyway.

"When I was a kid, twelve years old, my father was arrested for murder."

I widened my eyes. "Oh, my God!" I wasn't expecting that.

"Obviously he didn't do it. He was set up. Our family couldn't afford the legal fees that came with a murder case, so he was appointed an attorney through the court system. He was awful. He was there for his buck, and it didn't matter to this man if my dad was innocent or not.

"The case was over pretty quick. Dad pleaded not guilty, but the court didn't agree. He was found guilty and was sentenced to life without parole. A few years later, he died in his cell, stabbed to death."

"Oh, Chase," I whispered and reached for his hand.

He let me hold him as he continued. "About two years later, new evidence came forward that would have released my father from any accusations. But since he was already dead, there wasn't much they could do. The person whose DNA was found, though, was arrested for another murder. They had enough evidence to prove the man was guilty without using my father's case.

"A pardon was issued for my father. Although it was too late for my father, it cleared our family's name. Since that moment, I knew I wanted to be a defense attorney. I wanted to be able to help those who were falsely accused of crimes. The innocent. It's been a tough road but one I would do over and over again."

My heart bled for this man. I wanted to hold him in my arms and tell him I was sorry for his loss. He had to carry that on his shoulders, day in and day out.

"I'm sure your father is looking down on you now, proud of the man you've become," I told him.

"Maybe," he said. "Wow, that was heavy." He chuckled. "Tell me about you."

I blinked a few times. "Well, I haven't lived an exciting life, and I haven't experienced anything as you have. My life is pretty dull in comparison."

"Maybe I like dull. Go ahead."

I smiled and nodded. "One of my best friends in our school lost her father. He was murdered. The man who did it was found and tried and then put away. When it was time for his parole, it was denied. My friend fell into a life of depression, drugs, and prostitution. I tried many times to intervene, but it never helped. Eventually, I had to walk away. It was the hardest thing I ever had to do."

"I'm sorry to hear that," he told me.

"Thank you." I continued on. "Since I was a little girl, I wanted to be an attorney. I wanted to help those who needed it. I wanted to represent women who had been through hell and back and to protect their children."

"Because of what your friend went through?"

I nodded. "I saw a darkness in this world I never wanted to experience for myself."

My drink was brought over, and I stared at the contents, with three green olives speared with a metal stick. I picked it up and took a sip. "Thank you," I offered to the server, who returned a nod.

"Is that why you decided to represent the defense instead of the prosecution?"

"No, not exactly. I read many cases similar to yours and wanted to help make a change. However, I also wanted to prosecute the dirtbags responsible for the crimes they committed."

"Sounds like you're on the fence, then," Chase said.

"I think I still am, in a way, but I want to help people who can't help themselves. If that means representing them as a defense attorney, then that's what I'll do."

"Are your parents still alive?" he asked.

I nodded. "Yes. They're both in the Fort Worth area. I'm close with my mom, but my heart belongs to my daddy."

He grinned. "That's great to hear. My mom is still alive, but she's not in the best of health."

"Oh, I'm sorry to hear that."

"Thanks," he said and took a sip of his amber liquid. "She's in a nursing rehab home right now in Austin. She's had dementia for a while."

I wanted to hug him again. This man had been through so much torment in his life. It wasn't fair. Yet, here he was with me, smiling and enjoying himself.

"How do you do it?" I asked.

He pressed his brows together. "How do I do what?"

"All of this? Run your own firm? Smile? Live? Be out with me?" I felt I was rambling but didn't care. "You're like some kind of Superman, you know that?"

He chuckled. "There comes a time when you have to push everything you feel to the back burner and put your best foot forward. At some point, you have to put yourself first. If not, there's a chance you could hurt yourself in the process. Am I sad about my mother? Of course, but there's nothing I can do for her other than be there. The days she remembers me are the best days of my life. When I walk in and she screams because she has no idea who I am, it kills me a little more every single fucking time. So, Ainsley, you have to do what is best for you and put that foot forward and live. You must choose to live. You have only one life, and it's up to you what you do with it."

I felt my eyes burn as they watered with tears. "I don't know what I would do if it were my mom or dad." I shook my head and swiped at my tears. "I'm sorry. I don't mean to cry."

A white napkin was held in front of me. I smiled and took it.

"Thank you," I whispered.

"You're welcome," he said and slid closer on the couch. "Ainsley?"

I sniffed and set the napkin down. I met his gaze and felt my lips part. He was close, so close.

"I haven't told anyone that story about my mom, or my dad, in many, many years," he said. "What is it about you? Why do I trust you?"

I shook my head slowly. "I'm sure I don't know."

He leaned in a little more.

We were alone in this booth. No one would come in, and I'd be damned if we left.

"Chase," I whispered, and a rush of breath pushed past my lips.

"I want to kiss you," he told me. "Let me kiss you, Ainsley."

I licked my lips, and Chase groaned in approval. I wanted to touch his face, his chest, his back, feel his skin against my own. But not here.

He lifted his hand and cupped my cheek and then with the other, pushed a few strands of hair behind my ear. Cupping both sides of my face, Chase leaned in and slanted his lips across mine.

Instant fire and electricity shot through my body. It was as if I had been running idle and the touch of Chase brought me back to life with a bolt.

I placed my hands on his chest and moved them up to his neck, holding on to him.

He tilted his head and deepened the kiss, pressing his tongue against my lips, and I opened for him. His tongue sought mine and teased it.

I scooted closer to him. I wanted to straddle his lap, but I remained on the love seat instead.

Chase tilted my head and trailed his lips along my jawline to my ear. His breath was heavy in sensitive areas of my neck, and chills raced down my spine. A heat ignited between my legs, and I pressed my thighs together in an effort to extinguish it. God, I wanted him to touch me, taste me, be inside me, and claim me. I also knew we shouldn't do all of that here, in public. He was a prestigious attorney, and what was in his hands was my career. Not my body.

"Chase," I whispered. "We need to stop."

"I know we should," he said and nibbled on my ear, "but I can't find the strength to stop."

I gasped when he pulled me closer. He moved his arms around my body and dug his fingers into my skin.

I pressed my hands to his chest and put a small amount of space between us. "We need to stop," I whispered. "We're still in public."

With a sigh, he groaned and pulled away. Chase adjusting himself didn't go unnoticed. I smirked, enjoying the feeling that I'd done that to him.

"I want to see more of you, Ainsley."

I felt a giddiness overpower me, and a giggle managed to make its way out of my mouth.

He chuckled. "Shall we?" he asked and stood, offering me his hand.

I reached for it as a female's voice interrupted our private moment. "Ma'am, you cannot interrupt the party inside. You are not an invited guest."

"I don't care if it's the President of the United States! Get out of my way!"

CHAPTER TEN

CHASE

"Ainsley, sit down, please."

Rage bubbled to the surface, and I didn't want Ainsley getting hurt. Not that I would be swinging my arms, by any means, but this was not her fight.

The curtains were yanked back, and in barged Patricia, the faux *Monet.*

From a distance, she was striking, beautiful, exotic. Her long blond hair was loose in curls and tumbled down her back. Her bright-blue eyes were wide with shock when she stared into mine. She looked at Ainsley and me and then crossed her arms over her chest.

"What the fuck is this?" she demanded.

"I should be asking you the same thing," Ainsley growled.

"What do you want, Patricia?" I asked.

Before she barged into my office yesterday morning, the last time I saw her—outside of court—was her bedroom while she was getting fucked by my friend.

"I heard you were here, and well, I wanted to see you," she said.

There was the familiar whine in her voice she used to use with me. I'd found it cute when we first started dating, but eventually it grew to irritate me. She sounded like a fucking child.

"You're not welcome back here," the bouncer told her.

"Fuck off," she said to the man and turned back to me. "As I said, I'm here for you. But I can see you're here fucking another one of your whores."

"Excuse me?" Ainsley said and stood up.

"We're done here, Patrica," I said and then turned to Ainsley. "Please ignore her, Ainsley. Come on. I'll take you home."

"You're not going anywhere with her," Patricia ordered. "You're coming with me. You belong with me."

With a sigh, I lifted a brow and stared into Ainsley's eyes. "Give me a minute to take out the trash?"

She grinned. "Take your time. I still have my martini to drink."

I winked at her, and she giggled. How did I get so lucky finding this woman? Would just anyone have stood by my side while my ex talked trash? She was quite remarkable.

"I owe you one," I whispered.

"Hmm, I'll take you up on that." She sat down, lifted the olives from her drink, slid one off, and chewed it. She then lifted her gaze to mine and winked.

Sexy as hell.

"Come on, Chase," Patricia ordered. "Now. Let's go."

I turned back to Patricia. "Do like my friend here said and get out. You're not welcome here."

"Even after you fucked me the way you did? Oh, come on now, Chase. We both know we're made for each other. We're both bold and expect the same in someone else. I can handle you where no one else can." Her last words were directed to Ainsley.

Ainsley, in response, ate another olive and smiled.

My God, this woman surprised me tonight. I had no idea she had this much moxie. Sexy as fuck was what that was.

I sighed and placed my hands on my hips. "You need to leave, Patricia. Nothing will ever happen again between us. We're over, and you need to accept that."

Patricia gasped and stepped into the private room. She snatched Ainsley's drink from her and chucked it onto my chest. "Fuck you, Chase! Fuck you!" And then she turned and stormed out of the room.

The bouncer peeked in and shook his head. "Sir, I'm truly sorry. Everything will be comped and on the house tonight."

"I appreciate that," I told the man, "but please, it's not necessary."

The man nodded. "Yes, sir."

I wiped at my jacket and then turned to Ainsley. As she stood, I gaped at her dress. The front was now wet from the backsplash of her drink.

"Ahh hell, Ainsley. I'm sorry."

She looked at me and laughed. "Why are you sorry? This is by far the best date I've been on in a while. We opened up deep wounds, and I got to see the horrendous ex in her prime. I mean, she dumped my amazing martini on us, but to see you tell her off? Quite fun!"

I shook my head. "Where the hell have you been all my life? I think any other woman would have been completely offended by the turn of events."

"Well," she said and stepped closer to me, slipping her hands over my chest and wet jacket. "I'm not any other woman. I'm just me."

I grinned and cupped her cheek. I swiped my thumb under her bottom lip and then leaned in and kissed her softly on her lips.

"I'm very happy about that."

♦ ♦ ♦ ♦

I hadn't anticipated bringing Ainsley to my home tonight. The thought had crossed my mind, but I didn't think it would happen. Yet here we were. My driver pulled up my driveway and into my garage and then opened my door.

I stepped out and then offered her my hand. She accepted it and stood by my side. I looked over my shoulder to my driver. He bowed his head, lowered the garage door, and made his way out a side entrance.

Once the garage door was closed, I turned back to Ainsley. "Nervous?"

"After the show tonight? Not at all."

I chuckled. "I'm sorry that happened."

"So, who's Patricia *really*?"

I took her hand and led her into my home. Lights turned on as we stepped inside and closed the door behind us.

I shrugged off my suit jacket. "Let's say she's my worst mistake." I unbuttoned my sleeves, then began working on my dress shirt.

"Umm, Chase?" she asked.

"Yeah?"

"Are you undressing?" She was blushing.

I smirked and gave her a nod. "Absolutely. We're both soaked. Come on. I have a T-shirt and some boxers you can put on if you want?"

Her brows rose in surprise. "Am...well, am I staying here tonight or something?"

"Do you want to?"

She shrugged. "I hadn't thought that far ahead, actually."

She'd said she wasn't nervous, but that changed as soon as we talked about changing clothes and the possibility of her staying the night.

Damn, I wanted her in my bed. I want to wake her by settling between her legs and licking her delectable pussy.

"Tell you what. You can change, and then I'll have my driver take you home. Sound good?" My dick was hard and throbbed in my pants. I wanted to shower and take her with me. Push her against the tile and fuck her until the morning sun rose.

She nodded. "That'll work."

"Okay, follow me." I led her toward my bedroom, which was more rustic than the kitchen.

"I love your bed frame," Ainsley said.

I had a king-size bed with four light-pine columns that looked like smoothed trees.

"I appreciate that. It's from some of the land my family owns. I had it made."

She smiled, walked toward the bed a few paces, and then turned around.

"I want to shower and clean up. Care to join me?" I waggled my brows.

She laughed and shook her head. "I don't think that's such a great idea."

"Why not?" I asked. "I mean, we're both covered in martini. The least I could do is offer you the shower."

"Would I be alone in said shower?"

I smirked and stepped closer to her. I shook my head. "Not a chance."

She pursed her lips together. "I don't think it's a good idea."

"I agree," I started and lowered myself to my knees on the floor. "I think it's a *great* idea."

Ainsley grinned, and then a soft laugh left her. "You're incredible, you know that?"

"So I've been told." I loved her laugh, and she had an amazing smile. I scooted closer and pressed my chest to her knees. I rested my arms on her thighs and folded my hands. "I did have a great time tonight, regardless of Patricia."

"Patricia who?" she said with a wink. "I had a great time too. And Chase?"

"Yeah?"

She paused before speaking and slipped her hand through my hair. I closed my eyes and tilted my head into her caress and was startled a bit when she pressed her lips to my forehead.

"Thank you for opening up to me."

I lifted my gaze to hers. "Thank you."

Ainsley then moved her legs apart and allowed me to move in closer. My chest was now pressed to her sweet spot, the entrance to her body, her pussy. My dick throbbed even harder being this close to her.

She bent down and cupped my cheeks and then tilted my head up. She slanted her lips over mine and, sighing into my mouth, kissed me with a desperation I had never encountered. It was hard, passionate, and erotic.

I stood and pulled her to her feet without breaking our kiss. I felt along her dress for a zipper but only shoved my hands through the crisscross of the back of her dress.

I growled into her mouth. "Where's the fucking zipper?"

She grinned against mine. "On my left side."

"Duly noted." I felt along the side of her dress until I

found it. I pulled the zipper down and exposed her bare side.

Ainsley's fingers began working the buttons of my shirt and shoved it over my shoulders and down my arms.

I pulled the dress free from her body, and it dropped to a pile of black on the floor.

She stood before me in only black lace panties and her heels.

I took a step back and admired the beauty before me. She was exotic yet graceful and elegant, and her nipples hardened to the chill in the air.

Tonight, she was mine.

CHAPTER ELEVEN

AINSLEY

I had waited all my life for something incredible to happen. I had no idea that moment would be right now in Chase Newstrom's bedroom.

While he was down to his undershirt, pants, and shoes, I stood shivering from nerves and chill in only my panties and stilettos.

I felt exposed and folded my arms in front of my body.

"What are you doing?" he asked.

"I'm... I'm embarrassed," I whispered.

"About what? You're a beautiful woman."

I looked at the floor and felt tears build in my eyes. "I have a belly pouch. My legs are thick. I have a big ass. My boobs are huge. I've seen the women you take home, Chase. I'm not like them."

He pressed a finger to my chin and lifted my head. He looked into my eyes and smiled. It was sweet and filled with sincerity.

"You're here with me because you are not them, Ainsley. Your stomach is perfect. Your legs are strong and sexy as hell. Your ass... Damn, I want to bite it and get my hands on it. I want to squeeze it while you ride my cock. And your tits? Shall I go on about how amazing your tits are?"

I sniffed and let out a small laugh. "Yeah, let's hear about my tits."

He grinned. "I would titty fuck you in a heartbeat."

"Wow, you sweet talker you," I teased.

I knew what he was doing, and it was working. But that voice in my head still screamed at me to get my clothes on and get the fuck out. That Chase was too good for me. That I didn't deserve someone like him. My eyes drifted to the floor once more.

"What happened? Where did you go just now?" he asked. "You are a sexy, voluptuous goddess, Ainsley. Any man would give anything to be with you."

I laughed, then sniffed and wiped at my eyes. "Well, it's to hear you think that, Chase."

"I don't know what happened in your past with prior lovers, but you're here with me now. Don't let them invade your mind. It's just you and me." He stepped closer and cupped my cheeks. "Just us and no one else."

"Just us," I repeated.

"Yes," he whispered and pressed his lips softly to mine. "Just us. Let yourself go, Ainsley. Let go and give yourself to me."

"I . . . I don't know how to let go." My body tensed, and I wanted to run. Not because I didn't want to do this but because his very presence rocked me to my core. I was in danger of losing myself to this man, and when I did, there would be no going back.

"Let go," he whispered. "Let's have tonight."

"What about tomorrow?"

"I'll have you tomorrow then as well."

I giggled and looked into his eyes. Chase smiled and

rested his forehead against mine. "You're exquisite, Ainsley. I only wish you could see what I do."

"If we turned off the lights—"

"No," he said abruptly. "The lights will stay on. I want to look into your eyes when I claim you. I want you to know how goddamned sexy you are. I want you, Ainsley."

I felt a tear slip down my cheek. Chase caught it and swiped it away.

"I've got you, Ainsley. Now let yourself go."

My heart sped in rapid beats and my legs shook. I wanted him more than I'd wanted anyone in my entire life. I needed to feel his lips on me, his body against mine, his length pushing inside me.

"Chase," I whispered and lifted my head. My lips met his, and I reached for him. Gripping his hair, I pulled him hard against me.

He growled against my lips, slid his hands over my backside, and then gripped my ass with his palms, spreading me wide, just for him. My pussy ached for him.

"I need you," I whispered against his mouth.

"Then let me have you," he said.

"Take me," I told him. "All of me."

Chase let go of my ass and began working on his pants.

I grabbed his undershirt, pulled it off his body, and tossed it. His chest and abs were ripped, and I imagined running my tongue over the ripples of his muscles, like the waves of the ocean along his body.

He pushed his pants and boxers to the floor and stood. His cock pressed against my belly.

I reached between us and wrapped my hand around his length. He was thick and long, and the head of his cock had a bead of pre-come. I wanted to lick it in desperation.

"What are you doing to me, Ainsley?" he whispered. "I need inside you, woman."

"I want you," I whispered. "Please."

He groaned as I stroked his cock. The dampness on the tip of his head aided as a lubricant.

"Shower. Now," he ordered.

I grinned and continued to stroke him. "You feel so good in my hand, though."

"Oh, I'm positive I'm enjoying this more than you are."

I released him, and Chase let out a frustrated sigh.

"Let's go, woman. Before I explode all over you and my bedroom." He walked over to his nightstand and opened the top drawer. I couldn't see what was inside, but he pulled out a condom and then closed the drawer.

I laughed and followed him toward his bathroom. He had a large shower, big enough for at least four people. It had multiple showerheads, side showers, and it was enclosed with a glass wall. There was a jetted tub on the opposite side of the bathroom and a large vanity between.

Chase pushed open the shower door, stepped inside, and then turned the shower knobs.

When the sprays started, he turned to me with a grin. "Come on, beautiful." He placed the condom on one of the shelves in the shower.

Were we actually about to do this? Were we going to cross the threshold of no return? Every part of me screamed *yes*. I would have to worry about tomorrow later. Tonight, it was about us and exploring our needs.

I kicked off my shoes and pulled my panties down my body. When I stood, Chase held his cock in his hands and slowly stroked it. I removed my hair from the bun it was in, and it tumbled over my left shoulder.

He grinned and lifted a brow. He motioned with one finger to join him.

I stepped into his shower and closed the door behind me. Steam enveloped me before the water touched my skin.

Chase held his hand out for me, and I took it. He led me to where he stood and pulled me close, so close. Our naked bodies touched, and water streamed over us.

My hair grew wet and clung to my body. Chase slid his hands down my waist to my hips. He closed his eyes and pressed his forehead against mine. His lips were parted, and his breath rushed from them as his tongue darted out to wet his mouth.

"Touch me," I whispered.

His eyes opened and stared into mine. "I want to taste you."

I fisted my hands at my sides, and my body shook with need. I was afraid if he touched my clit, my breasts, anything, I would explode in a fiery inferno.

"I need you," I said.

Chase lifted his hands to my breasts and cupped the heavy mounds before pressing them together, his fingers teasing my nipples.

I closed my eyes, gasping.

"Look at me," he said.

And I did. Our eyes met once more, and then he dipped down and flicked his tongue over my pebbled skin. He sucked one of my nipples into his mouth and teased the other with his fingers. He then moved to the other one and dropped one of his hands down between my legs.

I moved my leg and balanced it on one of the lower shelves in the shower. He slipped his finger between the folds covering my clit and teased it.

My body bucked.

He sucked on my nipple and moved his finger in a back and forth action, fast, furious, hard, and needy.

My pussy clenched, and I tilted my head to the side. My leg holding my weight began to shake, but not from holding myself. It was from the oncoming orgasm Chase was conjuring in my body.

"Chase!" I bit back a scream, and my body shook as the threat of an orgasm called.

"Let go," he told me and stood tall over me, looking down into my eyes. With his free hand, he fisted it into my wet locks and yanked my head to the side. "Let go and scream my name, Ainsley." He dove down to my neck and licked the sensitive flesh under my ear.

He shoved his fingers into my pussy and moved them as if to say *come here.* He pressed his thumb to my clit and massaged it in rhythm with the finger-fucking he was giving me.

My body rocked against his hand, and with Chase's mouth on my neck and hand in my hair, I was going to lose myself.

"Chase!"

"Give it to me, baby," he growled in my ear. "Come on my hand. Give. It. To. Me." He enunciated each word as his fingers fucked me.

"Oh, shit, Chase!" I screamed as I held on to his shoulders. My orgasm ripped through my body, thrashing like a burning wildfire, and only his body could quench the flames.

"That's it, baby. Yes, give it to me." He moved his hand

with manic precision and then pulled his fingers free from my pussy. Just when I thought was he done, he surprised me by pinching my clit and rubbing the bundle of nerves between his finger and thumb.

"Chase, yes, oh, God!"" I screamed as another orgasm struck me. He pinched harder and continued to slide his fingers with my clit in his fingertips.

"You like that, baby?"

"Oh, God, yes!" My leg began to shake again. I would fall soon if we didn't stop.

Then Chase slipped his free arm around my body. "Put your leg down, baby," he said and let go of my clit.

My body shook as I looked at him through the steam of the shower. His eyes were a darker blue than they'd been before. His hair was wet on his head, his chest was slick, and his cock hard. I desperately wanted him in my mouth.

"Let me suck you. Fuck my mouth, Chase."

He grinned. "Soon, baby. Soon. First, I want to fuck that pussy of yours." He reached for the condom and ripped it open. He set the wrapper back on the shelf and then rolled the rubber onto his cock.

"Come here, baby," he said and took my hands. He held them above my head and gripped them with one hand. He grabbed one of my legs and wrapped it around his waist. He pressed his cock against me, rubbing it against my clit.

"Fuck me, please," I whispered. "I need you inside me."

He let go of my hands. "Hold on to me, baby."

I placed my arms around his neck and held on when he lifted my other leg. Chase pressed the head of his cock to my pussy and pushed.

I gasped, the size of him invading my core, stretching

me, filling me. He pulled back and pushed in once more.

"Are you okay?" he whispered.

I nodded. "Oh, yes, and don't you dare hold back."

He grinned and captured my lips again in a heated, desperate kiss. I was starving for him, and he was my sustenance, ready and willing to give everything he had to me. He pulled back and then pushed with a massive thrust. A scream erupted from me, and he did it again and again. Every push from Chase drove me closer and closer to the edge of eruption.

I'd had sex and I'd enjoyed myself, but I'd *never* had sex like this. Ever. I had always been in control of myself, my body, everything about me. However, in this moment, I lost myself and was happy to give every bit of control over to Chase. *Why fight it?*

"Yes, Chase, yes," I groaned and then leaned into his neck and nibbled on his ear.

"Fuck, woman, what are you doing to me?" He grunted hard with another thrust, and it was the sexiest sound I'd ever heard. "Fuck, you feel good, baby," he growled. "So good, so tight."

"Yes," I screamed into the space of the shower. The water continued to pour on our bodies as Chase pushed harder, thrusting with a force that would soon shatter me. Ruin me for anyone else.

"I'm going to come, Chase. Come with me, please."

"Oh, I'm close, baby, so close. So close." His pushing became faster, erotic, and hot. So fucking hot. He growled next to my ear. "Yes, baby, I'm coming. Come with me, Ainsley. Yes, now, baby, now!"

I screamed, my orgasm exploding through my body with

an intensity I had no idea I could experience. My body shook, and my breaths came in rapid bouts of air.

"Fuck," Chase groaned and held me against the wall for another moment before he slid free. He helped me get back to my feet and slid off the condom. He laid it with the wrapper and then washed his body free from the residue.

"Come here," he said. "Let me bathe you, baby."

I smiled, and my legs shook. "I don't know if I can." I laughed. "I can barely stand."

He chuckled and made his way to me. "Then I'll help you. Come on." Chase held on to me and stood me under one of the showerheads. He lathered up some soap and moved it over my body. The suds rinsed down the drain, and I wondered where this would leave us in the morning.

"Will you stay with me tonight?" Chase asked.

I met his gaze and smiled. "Yes."

He grinned an adorable lopsided grin. "Good," he said and kissed me softly on the lips. "I want to wake with you in my arms."

I pursed my lips together. Everything I thought Chase Newstrom appeared to be just an illusion. He bore his past about his father, stood by my side against his ex, and now, in his home, caressed me in suds. Chase Newstrom was nothing as he appeared.

And I was falling in love with this side of him.

CHAPTER TWELVE

CHASE

I yawned as the morning sun began its ascent over the land. Warmth enveloped my body, and when I opened my eyes, Ainsley Speire lay in my arms. Her back pressed into my chest, my hips into her bottom. I knew by the rhythm of her breaths she was still asleep.

I smirked as last night's events played back in my head. If someone had told me I would wake up in the morning with a beautiful woman named Ainsley Speire in my bed, I would have called bullshit. Yet here we were, and I needed more of her.

Her hair splayed over the pillow and her face. Gently, I took hold of the locks that lay across her cheek and moved them to the side. Her lips were parted slightly. She was beautiful as she slept.

My dick grew hard, and I pressed it against her ass. I reached over her body, hugged her to me, and grasped one of her breasts. The nipple responded immediately and grew taut against my palm.

Ainsley stirred and pushed back against me. She wasn't quite awake yet, but slowly, she was pulling from her slumber.

I slid my hand down the length of her smooth skin, over her belly, down to her thighs. I pulled her top leg back slightly, just enough to allow me to sink my fingers at the cleft of her pussy. I slid my finger over her clit and massaged it up and down, left and right, giving her a generous wake-up call.

Ainsley's breathing hitched, and she moaned a soft whisper and then reached for me, finding my neck. She pulled me close to her, and I nibbled on her ear.

"I want you," I whispered.

"You're doing just fine with my clit," she told me. She repositioned herself to her back, then opened her legs wider for me to play. But I needed more.

I moved down the bed and pulled the sheets over my head. Ainsley lay naked before me, and I wanted to touch, kiss, and lick every inch of her body. I feathered kisses from her waist to her hips. I felt her giggle, and I smiled.

"That tickles," she said.

I moved her leg closest to me around my body and then pushed her thighs open, far apart from one another. Ainsley was spread wide, just for me. She was an all-you-can-eat buffet, and damn if I wasn't hungry. I pushed the cleft of her pussy apart. She was wet and warm, her clit slightly red and swollen.

Giving her a tease, I slid my finger from the bud filled with thousands of nerve endings down to the entrance of her body. Her body shuddered, and a slight moan sounded from her.

"I want to hear my name on your lips," I told her. Before I gave her a chance to respond, I sucked her clit between my lips. I moved my hands under her hips and pulled myself closer to her. I wanted to bury my face against her body and taste every ounce of what she would give me.

Her hips moved against my face with each lash of my tongue. She tasted like the familiar plum I've grown to anticipate, long for, and desire. She was an addiction I never knew I needed until I tasted her for the first time.

"You're going to make me come," she groaned as she ran her fingers through my hair.

I sucked on her clit and hummed against her tender flesh. Her body bucked, and I held her firm against my mouth. Her honey spilled from her, and the taste was exquisite. The sweetest fruit, and I reveled in it. I needed more of her.

I moved an arm out from under her and pushed two fingers into her pussy. Ainsley's body squirmed and her panting grew louder. I sucked her harder and fucked her with my fingers. Harder, faster, more. I still needed more.

I pulled my fingers from her and licked her clean off my digits. I moved my fingers down to her puckered hole and pressed one of my fingers against her opening. As it slid inside, she gasped and tightened her grip on my hair.

"No one has ever . . ." She trailed off as I worked my finger farther inside.

"I promise it won't hurt." I pulled my finger back out slightly and then pushed it back into her ass. Her body was tense, and she needed to relax. The last thing I ever wanted to do was hurt her.

I sucked her clit back into my mouth as I moved my finger in and out of her hole. She opened her legs wider, and the chilled air suddenly hit my body. Ainsley pulled the covers from us, and she sat up on her elbows. She wanted to watch, and this hit me like overdrive. She wanted a show, and damn it if I didn't want to give her one.

With my other hand, I fingered her pussy, and Ainsley was close to becoming unglued.

"More," she groaned and rolled her head back. Her chest

heaved with heavy breaths, and her nipples grew harder while chills raced across her body. She was going to shatter soon.

Ainsley was close to orgasm. She just needed a harder push. As I flicked her clit with my tongue, she began to come on my fingers.

I pushed and pulled my finger in her ass, and while doing so, I removed the ones inside her core. Ainsley needed one hard fuck, one moment, that one over-the-edge hit to send her flying. She'd never had sex in her ass, but after this morning, she would beg for it.

I sat up on my elbow and looked up to her, meeting her gaze. "I told you I want to hear my name on your lips."

"Yes," she groaned and bit her lip. "I never knew ass sex could feel like this."

"Baby, this isn't ass sex. This is only playing."

She groaned again and opened her legs even wider. "Fuck me, Chase. Fuck my ass."

I smirked and continued moving my fingers. "Be careful what you're asking for. You're not quite ready for that yet, baby. Soon, I promise."

"I need to come, please, Chase."

I moved my finger in a circular motion in her tight hole, in and out, in and out. I moved it faster and harder. Ainsley gasped. Her legs shook and her hips bucked. Moving faster against her, I went from moving gently to pounding my hand against her ass.

"Fuck yes, Chase. Oh, hell, oh, my God!"

"Let go, baby. Just let go."

And she did. Ainsley shattered and arched her back. Honey creamed from her pussy and coated my hand. She was a goddess, and her giving herself to me like this, it was exquisite. It was the sexiest thing I'd ever witnessed . . . and I still wanted more.

I pulled my finger free from her and sat up to look down at her. "Good morning," I said with a smirk.

She grinned and laid an arm over her face before giggling. "Good morning." She peeked at me from under her elbow. She had a mischievous smile on her lips. "It's your turn now. I want to taste you. I want you to fuck my mouth."

My brows rose. "Well, I won't say no to that."

She sat up and leaned toward me. "I could wake up every morning like this."

A pain in my chest erupted. I wasn't sure if it was the truth clamping on my chest or guilt for knowing I may not be able to give her what she wanted. Because I wanted her. Hell, I needed her. Why was it now that I realized it and not when she first started working as an intern at my firm? Was I that shallow of a bastard?

Yes, yes I was. *Hello, Chase. Meet your ego, you self-centered son of a bitch.*

I pushed my self-hatred thoughts to the side and moved off the bed. I stood while Ainsley repositioned herself sideways across the mattress. Her head lay tilted over the edge of the bed, and her naked body was like a beautiful piece of art before me.

She reached for me and grasped my thighs, pulling me close to her. My cock touched her lips, the pre-come smearing across her mouth. She opened for me and pulled me even closer.

How in the hell did this woman even exist?

I didn't deserve her, did I? Fuck no, but I would work to earn her and the right to call her mine.

My dick slid inside her mouth, and when she closed her lips around my length, I groaned, pleasure rocketing down to my balls. Reaching down to her neck, I cradled her head and then began to push in and out, thrusting against her mouth. I felt the back of her throat and moved faster, more erratic. I closed my eyes, and for a moment, I forgot it was her mouth I was fucking and not her pussy.

My balls tightened as my own orgasm was coming. "Fuck, Ainsley!"

She groaned around my cock, and the vibrations sent me over the edge. I came hard and hot, and she didn't hesitate to take it all.

I grunted one final thrust. I pulled free from her mouth, and she rolled to her side. I pressed my palms into the mattress and glanced over to her.

She sat up like the lady she was, and with the tip of her finger, she dabbed at the corners of her mouth.

I chuckled and moved next to her as she stood. She ran her hands through her hair and then met my gaze.

I held it for a moment, looking into her hazel eyes. There were specks of gold and white in her irises. Her lids were framed with long black lashes. Her lips were slightly swollen and beautiful.

"Come on and clean up with me," I said.

She grinned with a nod.

I took her hand and led the way.

◆ ◆ ◆ ◆

I wasn't sure how long Ainsley and I were in the shower, but it was long enough that the hot water began to turn cold.

Maybe it was time for a tankless heater. Never-ending hot water sounded perfect right now.

I stepped out first and towel-dried my body. I hung a towel over the glass shower door for Ainsley and watched her body through the fogged glass of my shower. She was so different from the women I normally found myself with, and this was quite possibly why I was completely attracted to her.

Many wanted what they couldn't have, but once they had it, the want and need diminished. But this wasn't the case. I'd had Ainsley now, and it felt like I couldn't get enough of her. She matched my personality in many aspects and was one of the few who would call me on my shit.

And I respected her for that.

Most women I took home clung to every word I said, but they were only pretending to understand what I was talking about. I could have said the King of Pluto was coming to visit, and they would have believed me. There was never a connection on an intellectual or emotional level, and sex without emotion would never be more than just sex.

Sex with Ainsley was more.

I couldn't quite put my finger on it yet, but some heavy feelings were involved. I couldn't call it the L-word. Frankly, that word freaked me the fuck out. The only woman I'd ever loved was my mother. I once thought I could have loved Patricia, but she had been more in love with my money and social status than me.

The shower was still running, so I left the bathroom to give Ainsley a few minutes to herself. I was wrapping a bath towel around my waist when my doorbell rang.

Who would be here this early? There was the annual charity event coming up soon, so maybe someone was bringing information by? I was a supporter, after all.

I quickly threw on some boxers and khakis and made my way to the front door. I peeked through the peephole to see who it was, but a manila envelope blocked my view. I gritted my teeth.

With a sigh, I opened the door, and on the other side was Patricia. I gritted my teeth even harder. "What are you doing here?"

She pushed past me and walked into my home. "I have the tickets for us to the charity event."

"You're not welcome here, Patricia. You need to leave."

I kept the door open and stood next to it. Was her name still on the list the guard shack had? I would need to update that immediately.

Her eyes went from my face, down my body, and then back up again.

I felt completely exposed.

"As I said, I have the tickets for us to attend," she said. "We are going together, Chase. Don't deny me this event. It's huge, and all the right people will be there."

"No, Patricia. I'm not going with you. You need to leave, now, before I call the police to have you escorted out. You're now trespassing."

"Oh, come on, baby. You miss me. I miss you. I still love you, Chase." She made her way over to me and tried to push against the door to close it.

I kept my hand on it. "You need to leave. How many more times do I need to tell you I don't want you here?"

She then laid her hands on my chest and pushed up on her toes. "You miss my mouth on your dick, don't you?"

"Get the fuck out. Now." I grabbed her by the arms and

held her back. "Goodbye, Patricia." I moved her toward the door, and she wrangled out of my grip.

"Damn it, Chase! Don't do this. You and I belong together. We're both eager to win all the cases that come our way. We're winners, you and me. We fight for what we want, and I'll fight for you until there's no fight left in me."

"Is that what you told Mitch?"

She growled. "Damn it, Chase. Don't you see why I'm here? I accept you, flaws and all."

"What's going on?"

Patricia and I both turned to find Ainsley stepping out of my bedroom.

Ainsley's eyes widened when she saw me shirtless with Patricia's hands on my bare chest.

I quickly moved out of Patricia's reach. "You need to leave, Patricia. Now."

"Why is she here?" Patricia asked. "Fucking the help?"

I grabbed her arm and led her toward the door.

"How dare you," Ainsley yelled toward her. "You don't know me or why I'm here."

"Oh, don't I, though?" Patricia returned. "Oh, did Chase tell you why he became a lawyer?"

"Patricia, don't," I warned her. "You need to go."

"Yes, as a matter of fact, he did," Ainsley said. "Now, I think he's asked you a few times already to leave."

Patricia's eyes widened. "Did he tell you about his secret from high school?"

My heart fell into the pit of my stomach. I never wanted to relive that moment. Telling Patricia about my past had to have been the worst mistake of my life. I had no idea she was going to hold it over my head.

"What?" Ainsley asked. She looked at me and then back to Patricia.

"In high school, Chase took some girl out on a date and ended up being accused of rape. What do you think happened, Ainsley? Was he completely innocent, or did he abuse his power? You know, his pretty face, all that money, nothing to lose while others might have everything to lose... Does any of this feel familiar to you right now?"

I fisted my hands by my sides. I didn't care if Patricia was a woman or not. I pushed her out of my home and slammed the door.

With a sigh, I turned back to Ainsley. Her face was no longer the peaceful calm image of the woman I woke up to this morning. No, now her face grew redder by the second. Her arms shook, and she closed her eyes.

I took a few steps toward her. Before I reached her side, she held a hand up.

"No. Don't bother." Her voice was low yet demanding, like a trainer working with her dog.

And in this scenario, I was absolutely the dog.

"Ainsley, please let me explain."

She opened her eyes and met my gaze. I felt a heat coming from her stare, and it wasn't welcoming or warm.

"I would never hurt anyone vulnerable, Ainsley. The girl dropped her case immediately, and my name was cleared. Patricia is right about one thing only. That *is* what caused me to pursue a career in law."

Ainsley didn't say anything. She turned, went back into my bedroom, and closed the door behind her.

I was locked out of my own bedroom. This was not how I expected this day to turn out... at all.

CHAPTER THIRTEEN

AINSLEY

I held on to the bedroom doorknob for a moment and closed my eyes.

Numb... I was numb, but I felt my mind spiraling. My stomach lurched, and I pressed my hand over my mouth. I ran as fast as my feet would carry me to the bathroom and heaved over the toilet. Nothing came up since I hadn't eaten or drunk anything, but it didn't stop me from trying.

Everything came rushing at once. From the time I started work at Chase's firm to the moment his ex walked out of his home, it all came crashing down.

I was that woman. I'd fucked my boss. I'd fucked my motherfucking boss.

I dry heaved again. Once it passed, I pulled at the toilet paper and blew my nose. My body shook as I began to cry.

Who am I?

This wasn't me. I would never make such a mistake that it would cost me the career I had always dreamed of and was just starting to build.

If it weren't for his ex catching me here... If it weren't for Chase being so incredibly hot... If it weren't for me drinking that fucking Scotch that night...

This was all my fault. I had no one to blame but myself.

My chest ached with the realization of what had just occurred, and I longed for the magic pill that would allow me to turn back time.

"Ainsley?" Chase was at the bedroom door.

"Go away."

Where would he go? I was at his house, in his bathroom, attempting to lose myself inside his toilet. If my parents could have only seen me now, they would have been so disappointed in the person I'd become.

"The heart wants what the heart wants," my mother once told me. Her voice echoed in my mind over and over, like a broken record.

"Ainsley, I'm going to come in," Chase warned.

I tossed the toilet paper into the toilet and flushed it. I wiped at my eyes, removing the evidence of my tears. He didn't deserve to see the pain he'd caused. He didn't deserve to see me at my worst. Chase didn't deserve me.

The bedroom door opened, and tentatively, he stepped through. His stance was stiff, like a man walking through a minefield in a war zone. I supposed, in a way, he was doing just that.

"Are you all right?" he asked.

I shook my head. "No, Chase, I'm not all right." I left the bathroom and gathered up anything of mine that could be shoved into my purse. I needed to leave and get him out of my sight. My skin began to itch, and my heart raced.

"I'm sorry about Patricia—"

"You don't get to do that!" I yelled as I crossed the room to where he stood, finger pointed to his face.

He frowned. "Come again?"

"No, you don't get to do that," I started. Anger rose, and I felt the ammunition of it heat my cheeks. "You don't get to tell me you're sorry about the assbag who just graced us with her presence. You don't get to feel sorry for yourself because we were caught fucking. You don't get to sit here and pretend like I'm not your intern who just ruined her own career, Chase."

"Whoa, I don't know what happened—"

"I'm not done!" I shook my head and began to pace in his bedroom. Everything that had happened between us blew up in my face. "The night I wrote you that note was the worst mistake I have ever made. You are so fucking inconsiderate! Do you know that?" I stopped pacing and looked him in the eyes. "Let's see if I can help you understand what I see, maybe give you some perspective. I worked my ass off to get to where I am. I shaved a year off college by doubling up. I built a strong reputation for myself, and look where that got me. It's ruined, Chase. It's all for nothing."

"Ainsley, stop, please. Let me talk."

"No." I stepped into his space. We were almost nose-to-nose, and his scent invaded me. Hell, he smelled so good. I wanted to devour him—angry sex to show him what he did that was so wrong. But it wasn't him, not all of it. Most of everything that happened was because of me. It was that truth that killed me, that hurt the most, that would haunt me the rest of my days.

"Sleeping with you was a mistake, Chase. Giving myself to you was the worst thing I could have done. No one will ever take me seriously, and I guarantee you that whore-mouth ex of yours is calling everyone she knows right now to share that tidbit of news."

I turned away from Chase to pick up my purse, but he grabbed my arm.

He turned me back to face him and cupped my face. He stared into my eyes and passed his thumbs over my cheeks.

"Don't do this," he whispered.

"It's already done." I pulled his hands away. "Don't follow me," I told him and turned away. I pulled my hair back and wiped at my face to remove any stray tears. I couldn't bring myself to look at Chase before I left. I needed to get out of here, get space between us, and figure out my next steps.

I knocked on the wood-grained door and waited. The door pulled back, and the familiar face I needed to see smiled at me. My trust, my safe space, my home, my mom.

I tried to smile, but everything I had been holding in came rushing out in an onslaught of new tears. Sobs broke free, and I covered my face, ashamed of myself.

"Ainsley?" my mom questioned and pushed open the screen door. She pulled me into the safety of her arms. It was a place I loved to be, regardless of the circumstances. My mom's embrace would chase away the nastiest demon and bring peace to anything I felt.

I already felt better just by letting myself cry on her shoulder. She ushered me inside and closed the door.

"Phil, put on some tea. Ainsley is here. We'll be a few minutes," my mom called to my dad.

"You got it," my dad called back. "Welcome home, baby girl."

"Come on," Mom said and led me toward the guest bathroom. "Let's get you cleaned up. Tell me what happened."

Mom closed the toilet lid, and with another sob, I sat

down on it. I looked up to her and found her concerned eyes watching me. She had mended me from scraped knees to my first broken heart. She had been there to support me through my decision to go to law school and was always the voice of reason.

My mother was my best friend, and I was scared to death that she would be disappointed in me when I told her what I'd done. And I couldn't lose her friendship.

But I had to tell her.

"Mommy," I started, and she lowered herself to her knees.

She took my hands in hers and kissed my knuckles. "Talk to me, Ainsley. Let me help."

"I'm a horrible person," I started and then explained what had happened with Chase, the note, and our tryst. When it was over, I looked into her eyes and was relieved to find concern, not disappointment.

"Do you love him?" she asked.

My bottom lip trembled, and I nodded.

"Oh, honey," she said and pulled me to her.

And with that, I held on to my mother and cried on her shoulder.

"I think I ruined my career just as it was starting."

"No, darling," she said and pulled back to look into my eyes. "You're just getting your feet wet. Don't worry about this. We all make mistakes in our careers."

"But that's just it, Mom. My head is telling me it was a mistake, but I'm not sure being with Chase *was* a mistake."

"How does he feel?"

I shrugged. "I didn't exactly give him a chance to tell me before I ran out on him."

"What's your plan, then? Will you stay at his firm?"

I shook my head. "No. There's no way I can with this history between us now. I need to put in my notice and pray someone else will take me on." This brought me back to my concerns about Patricia. "I only hope that ex of his won't go blab her mouth all over town and make me look like the loose cannon she suspects I am."

"Being a loose cannon isn't all so bad. A loose woman who gives a turn like a doorknob? Well, that's totally different."

"Mom!" I exclaimed.

"What? It's the truth. But honey, you are not that woman. You are a strong, independent woman who goes after what she wants. There's nothing wrong with that. It's a great quality to have."

"Even if said quality slept with my boss?"

"You said you love him. As I've always said, the heart wants what the heart wants."

I let go of a long sigh and stood. I took my mom's hands and helped her to her feet and then embraced her.

"Thank you," I whispered.

"You're welcome."

We stood in the bathroom, hugging each other a moment longer, and then I let her go. "I need ice cream."

She smiled and brushed my hair behind my ears. "Chocolate or cookies and cream?"

CHAPTER FOURTEEN

CHASE

What the hell had happened? Had I fucked something up? I didn't quite understand why, but Ainsley was hell-bent on making me pay for something. She'd left abruptly and slammed the door in her wake.

Sleeping with you was a mistake.

The words echoed over and over in my mind. I sat on the edge of my bed, elbows on my thighs, and gripped the bridge of my nose. Sleeping with Ainsley was no fucking mistake.

My chest ached. It was unfamiliar, and I wanted it to stop. My stomach felt like I'd eaten something foul, but there was nothing in it. Just an empty void.

"Like my life," I muttered. My phone chimed on my nightstand. Hopeful it was Ainsley, I picked it up, disappointed to see it was a text from my brother, Brice. I slid my finger over the screen to read the message.

Hey, brother. Congratulations on your latest win. Let's celebrate! Can you come by later today at the house? I'm cooking steaks in your honor.

Sure, man, sounds good.
Be there around noon.

It sounded really good. I needed to get out of here, and spending time with my brother would be exactly what I needed to get out of this funk, get out of my own head. I needed to think clearly about what to do about Ainsley.

We hadn't been together long—hell, were we actually *ever* together?—but it was unlike anything I'd ever experienced. She had this way about her. She was a force to be reckoned with. No holding back, check-your-balls-at-the-door mentality. And I loved it.

I was never one to be serious with women and was always in charge. The Alpha, never the Omega. Even as siblings growing up, Brice had stepped back and let me make all the calls. It was probably why he worked for another law firm. He wouldn't be able to stand by while I ran the show, getting all the glory.

But it was never about glory. It was about standing up for those who were innocent.

♦ ♦ ♦ ♦

I brought the beer bottle to my lips and took a pull. The ice-cold liquid went down smooth. It was exactly what I needed. It was fall in Dallas, which honestly meant nothing. It was more like a second summer. It was hot and humid, but at night, it cooled to seventy-five.

The smell of the steaks made my stomach growl in hunger. I hadn't eaten anything all morning and hadn't wanted to after Ainsley left.

Sleeping with you was a mistake.

Somehow, somewhere, I had fucked up. But how? What the hell had I done?

"Again, brother, congratulations on the Vanderbilt case," Brice said as he turned the steaks on the grill.

"It was an open-and-shut case. The newest up-and-coming lawyer in my firm did the majority of the legwork. She was amazing."

I thought back to the moment when I had walked in on her in my office passed out from Scotch, the love/hate note tucked under her arm. She was sinfully sexy, but it took that note about how she felt to open my eyes. I was such a fool.

Brice put the grill fork down and turned to face me with brows raised.

"What?" I asked.

"Do tell. What's her name?"

I chuffed and took a swig of my beer. "No idea what you're talking about," I mumbled and turned away from him.

Heels struck the concrete patio, and I looked up to my sister-in-law, Madeline. She met my gaze and smiled. She was always dressed up as if she were about to entertain at any given moment. Today she wore a pink sundress and heels. She was beautiful, with long chestnut-brown hair, and I understood the attraction my brother had for her. They'd met while he was in law school, and the two had been inseparable ever since.

"Oh, did you meet someone?" Madeline asked.

"No. Yes. It's complicated," I said and took another drink. "I don't want to talk about it."

"All right," she said as she brought over vegetables in aluminum foil to grill. She handed them to Brice, kissed his cheek, and then headed back inside.

"You sure there's nothing to talk about?" Brice asked once we were alone again.

I sighed and took a seat on one of the patio chairs. "How

do you know you're in love?"

Brice chuckled as he tested the steaks and then put the vegetables on the grill. "You just know. It's not a sign or something someone can tell you. And saying 'I love you' doesn't mean you're in love. People use it so loosely nowadays. Tell me what happened."

I shook my head. "I have no idea where to start."

"How about the beginning?" Brice offered and closed the grill lid. He came over and took a seat next to me. He sipped on his beer and sat quietly, patiently.

Sitting and listening was what we did best. We listened to our clients to learn and understand, and then we defended. It was our livelihood. And I excelled at it. But telling my brother what was going on through my head?

I wrung my hands and felt my throat close up. "I feel like I can't breathe. The world is closing in around me. I can't function without her. And I somehow managed to fuck things up just as they were getting started."

Brice lifted a hand over his mouth, and his body shook as he chuckled.

"What the fuck, man?" I asked accusingly. "Seriously?"

"I'm sorry, bro, but you're Chase Newstrom. You never let a woman get under your skin. They get in your bed and then are on their way. How did this one get to you?"

I explained my walking in on her passed out and the note and everything that had happened since then, including this morning with Patricia.

"So I don't know what to do, how to act, or what I did to fuck it up."

"Well, for one, she met the ex. Never a good way to start unless you and the ex are good friends, and there's nothing,

MISADVENTURES WITH A LAWYER

at all, between the two of you."

"I can't stand the air Patricia breathes," I grumbled.

"Yeah, I can imagine. So she blew up at you this morning in your home when Patricia helped herself inside?"

I nodded. "Yeah." Then I took a drink.

"And you two had just come out of the shower?"

I nodded again. "What are you getting at?"

"Think for a moment about how it looked to Patricia."

"I couldn't give a fuck what Patricia thinks."

"No, not that. Think about what Patricia saw. Ainsley is your new protégée. You two were freshly showered and in your home, early in the morning. Imagine how Patricia saw Ainsley in this scene. Her imagination probably ran wild with the scenarios in her head."

It hit me like glass shattering on my skull. "Motherfucker." I groaned and closed my eyes.

"Yeah, you're welcome. You've got some cleanup and groveling to do."

"How did this even happen?" Hell, I knew how it happened. Fucking Patricia was how. She saw us together and would run wild with the news.

"You stuck your dick in her?" Brice said.

I frowned. "Fuck off." I rubbed at my forehead. "How do I save someone's reputation before it's even been created?"

"It's what we do, brother. Make a case for her, and go in like a knight on his horse."

I chuckled. "You haven't met Ainsley. She would kick my ass if I rode in like that. Trust me, she's the princess in the tower, but she's got a sword and she'd slay any dragon who tried to keep her locked away."

"Even better," he said and finished his beer. "Let me get

the steaks and veggies off. We'll eat, and I'm sure Madeline can help you make an action plan on how to grovel most effectively. I've had plenty of experience doing it myself."

I chuckled and stood with my brother. We didn't see eye-to-eye on many things, but I loved him regardless. He was there for me when I needed someone, and I could only hope to return the favor one day.

"Assuming this works out in your favor," Brice started, "I'll begin planning the bachelor party. *The* Chase Newstrom is smitten. Who would have ever thought?"

I grinned. I was taken by this woman and loved everything about it. I needed Ainsley Speire in my life. Even if it meant getting on my knees and begging for mercy, I would do it.

I was in love for the first time, and it scared the hell out of me. As a person who usually controlled everything in his life, I had no control whatsoever over this. It was exhilarating yet exhausting.

"How do you do it?" I asked.

"What do you mean?" Brice returned.

"Fall in love. Stay in love. Remain with one person for the rest of your life? How do you do it?"

"Very carefully and one day at a time. You'll go through hell and back, Chase. They will be your rock, and you'll be theirs. You'll see the best and worst of this person, and they'll know you better than you know yourself. And one day, you'll realize, you don't remember life before they came into it, and you'll never want to experience life without them."

"I've never wanted that for myself."

"And now?" he asked.

I met his gaze and rubbed the back of my neck. "I can't lose her, man."

"Then don't let her get away. You have the charity ball coming up, right?"

I nodded. "Yeah, it's soon. I wanted Ainsley to go with me."

"Did she agree to go?"

"I don't think I ever asked. I just said, 'she's going with me' to Patricia."

"Don't ever assume a woman will do what you tell her," Brice said.

I heard Madeline laugh behind me. I turned to find her watching us, a smug look on her face.

"How long have you been standing there?" I asked.

She shrugged. "Long enough to realize Chase Newstrom has a soul."

I chuckled. "Love you too, sis."

Madeline was a good person. I wasn't too crazy about her at first. If no one was good enough for me, the same rule applied when it came to my brother. But she'd ignored me and pursued Brice. And I was glad she did. She'd been an incredible addition to our family.

"Just tell her how you feel. If you love her, tell her. And don't be above groveling."

"Oh, there will be groveling," I said with a chuckle. "Just how much groveling, I'm not sure yet."

"You'll need to bring your A-game, brother," she said. "You'll need to give her enough to listen to your reason for begging for forgiveness. And even then, give her more. Let her know you fucked up, and beg her to tell you how to fix it." She looked over to Brice and then continued. "I don't like having to tell Brice when he fucked up or how to fix it, but in time, he figures it out." She returned her attention to me. "Let her be her own person. Don't try to control her."

I shook my head. "That will never happen. There's no way I could control her even if I tried! She's one of the strongest women I've ever met. I just wish I had seen sooner what I see now."

"You wouldn't have been ready," she told me.

The conversation I had with Ainsley came back.

"Funny, Ainsley told me the same thing."

"Smart girl," Madeline said with a wink. "I already like her."

Brice handed me a plate with a steak on it. "Come get some vegetables. You're going to need your energy."

I nodded and accepted the plate. The steak smelled amazing.

I knew I would need to get my A-game on to slay the theoretical dragon keeping her in the theoretical tower. The thing was, the tower was of her own making. I needed to get through to her before I lost her forever.

I had a fight on my hands for the love of my life. But I hadn't lost a case yet, and I wasn't about to start now.

CHAPTER FIFTEEN

AINSLEY

Wearing my old college T-shirt and pajama shorts, I sat on my couch and took another spoonful of my cookies and cream ice cream. My apartment was small, but it was mine. My feet were tucked under me, and the socks I wore were somewhere between half on and half off.

I was watching the latest baking reality show, and everyone was competing to make the best Halloween cake. They were being timed, and honestly, the pressure would be too much for me. Two hours to design and bake a cake? It took hours to prepare wedding cakes, sometimes days. Yet these people were expected to complete a masterpiece in two hours.

I shoved another scoop of ice cream into my mouth and sighed in contentment. I hated everything about today. My stupid heart was breaking, and my career was over before it even started, thanks to me putting out and that fucking whore, Patricia, walking in on us.

Who did she think she was, just walking into someone's home like that? Was there still something between her and Chase?

Who the fuck cared, anyway? He and I were over. Not like we were actually together to begin with, but I liked him. A lot. It should take weeks, if not months, to fall in love with someone, but with Chase, it felt like we had skipped past everything and jetted right into falling in love.

And I hated myself for it. Why had I gotten drunk on his Scotch and written that stupid note?

"Ugh," I groaned and took another bite.

"One hour left, bakers," the host announced on the TV program. One of the women was about to lose her shit, and she began to cry. Her cake was falling apart, the icing wasn't staying on, and she looked like she was about to throw in the towel and walk away. I could relate to this baker on a very serious level.

When a knock at my door sounded, I didn't want to answer it. I didn't want to see Chase. Hell, I didn't want to see anyone. The person knocked again.

"Delivery for Miss Ainsley...umm, Spear?" called the delivery man as he tried to pronounce my name.

I groaned and put my ice cream down. "Speire, like *ire*," I announced when I answered the door. "It's not hard." I looked at the delivery man, who held a large white box. I frowned. "What the hell is this?"

"No idea. I'm only delivering it, ma'am." He held out a clipboard for me to sign. I scribbled my name on it and looked to see who it came from, but there was no return address information. "Can you tell me who sent it?"

"Nope," the guy said and laid the box on its side and then turned to leave. He couldn't be older than twenty-one.

"How about a lesson in manners?"

"Yes, ma'am," the guy said as he took off.

I bent down and picked up the box. It wasn't heavy. I closed the door behind me and brought it to my small kitchen table. I pulled a chair out and took a seat. Staring at the box,

I had a sinking suspicion it came from Chase. The ball was coming soon.

"He would never do something like this."

I scooted out my chair and looked around my quaint kitchen. I'd decorated it with flying pigs. I loved the idiom *when pigs fly.*

I grabbed a set of scissors, went back to the box, and slid the sharp edge under the tape. I sat the scissors down and then slid the box open. I looked down on black tissue paper. It had a silver label over the middle that read *Prada.*

I chewed on my bottom lip. Prada? I'd never owned anything Prada and definitely couldn't afford it. I bought anything designer off the Poshmark application on my phone. Since discovering this little piece of heaven, I've been able to buy shoes and handbags from major designers at a fraction of what they'd cost in a store.

With a tentative finger, I broke the Prada seal and pulled the tissue paper apart. Inside was a folded dark-crimson dress made of satin and tulle. I lifted it from the box and found it had one shoulder. The other was bare. It had a line of roses adorning the one shoulder and a zipper along the side of the dress. It was fitted on top and flowed out from the waistline. It was absolutely stunning—and probably the most expensive piece of material I had ever held in my hands. And that included the title to my car.

I laid it back in the box and noticed a note in an envelope and a black shoebox, again labeled *Prada.*

Inside was a pair of black peep-toe stilettos that slipped on and had a diamond bowtie over the outer side of each shoe. They were gorgeous, and I was scared to wear them for fear of getting them dirty.

I laid the box to the shoes back down and picked up the note. I didn't see a name or anything inscribed on the outside. I opened it and pulled out a small slip of paper. I recognized the handwriting immediately.

Please forgive me. I'm an idiot and a tool. I'm so sorry.

Yours always,

Chase

My eyes burned with tears, and I let the card drop, fluttering down until it landed on top of the dress. I dropped into the chair and closed my eyes. A tear slipped down my cheek.

"Why the fuck did he do this?" I sat back in the chair and pinched the bridge of my nose. "Why? For fuck's sake, let me be mad for at least a fucking minute!"

I pushed the box away as if pushing away an empty plate. I wasn't full—in fact, I was starved for more of Chase—but right now there was no way I could stomach the mere presence of him.

I heard my phone chime the announcement of an email.

"That fucker better not have emailed me, too," I said and stood from my chair. I went to my bedroom and turned on the light. My room was about the size of my living room and held a queen-size bed, my dresser, and a desk. My legal books were stacked on end like a set of encyclopedias, and in front of them was my laptop. When my email loaded, my breath left my lungs.

It was from the bar exam. My results were in. This was it. Had I passed or failed?

My hands shook as I moved the mouse and clicked on the email. I saw my name, along with *Click here to get your results,* followed by the electronic signature from the dean of the school. I bit on my lower lip, closed my eyes, and clicked the link.

What if I'd failed? Would I take the exam again? Probably, but the fact that I'd failed the first time would follow me everywhere I went. How would I explain this? *Sure, I'll represent you, and, oh, yeah, I failed the bar the first time.*

But what if I'd passed? I couldn't wait any longer. I opened my eyes.

TEXAS BAR EXAMINATION RESULTS

Dear Ms. Ainsley Speire:

Congratulations on passing the Texas Bar Exam! We have certified you to the Supreme Court of Texas as eligible for licensure as a Texas attorney . . .

I gasped and stood from my chair so quickly, it toppled over and hit the hardwood floor with a bang. I covered my mouth and bounced on my toes with a squeal. *I passed! I fucking passed!*

I spun in a circle and ran in place for about twenty seconds. I laughed and shot my hands into the air in excitement.

"Fuck yeah! I need to call Mom!" I ran out of my room and grabbed my phone. I selected her speed dial button and brought the phone to my ear.

"Hey, darling," she answered.

"Mom!" I exclaimed.

"What's wrong?" she questioned immediately, fear in her

tone. "Are you all right? Where are you?"

"Mom, I'm fine. Hell, more than fine! Mom, oh, my God," I squealed. "I passed the bar!"

"That's amazing! I knew you could do it! Honey," my mom called out to my father, "she passed the bar."

"That's great, baby girl. I knew you would," I heard my dad call out.

I couldn't stop smiling. The pain I felt earlier from Chase was still there, but it was pushed to the back of my mind while the news of my bar result took prominence.

"So, what are your plans, then?" Mom asked.

"What do you mean?"

"Well, do you plan to stay with Chase, or are you going to go to another firm? Do you want to keep with defense or maybe become the district attorney someday?"

I had thought I wanted to be the DA for the first part of my college career and then thought better of it. I instead wanted to help those who couldn't help themselves. I wanted to be the voice for those who didn't have one.

"I don't know yet," I said, and it was the truth. "I don't know if I want to stay a defense attorney or go work for the county. I thought I knew, but now?"

"What about Chase?" she asked.

I rolled my eyes. "What about him?"

"Honey, you need to decide what you want. His feelings are at stake, too."

"Speaking of, you want to know what that asshat did?"

"Language, honey," my mom said.

"Sorry," I said under my breath. "He sent me an evening gown, Mom. Who does that?"

"A man who loves his woman, that's who," she said. "Your

dad never did anything like that for me."

"Like what?" I heard Dad call.

It made me giggle under my breath. Now, Mom would hold Dad to the standard of delivering her a dress, or flowers, or something.

"When's the last time you sent me something?" she asked him.

"Umm… Is this like the *does this make my butt look big* question?"

I laughed into the phone. "Leave Daddy alone." I stepped out of my room and looked across the way to the kitchen, where the dress sat in the box. With his note. "What do I do?"

"What do you want to do?" she asked.

"I want to feel like a pretty princess going to the ball. I want to find my Prince Charming and then kick him in his balls."

My mom laughed. "Well, that's not quite what I expected, but give him hell, honey. Make him work for that apology."

"That's assuming I forgive him."

"If you're considering going, the forgiveness has already started."

My mom had a point. I could wear the dress and not be his date though, right? No, that would be bad form. And rude. Basically, I would be Chase.

I sighed and sat back in the desk chair. "How does he manage to take my breath away when he's not even here?" I asked.

"Because, baby girl, you're in love."

"No, I'm not," I argued. "Love wouldn't put you in a position for all to see you're sleeping with your boss."

My mom sighed into the phone. "Honey, did you consider

he had no idea the other woman was coming by? Do you really think it was his intention to sabotage you?"

I shook my head, but it wasn't like she could see me. "No, Mom, I don't."

"Then maybe cut him some slack."

"I'm your daughter, remember? I don't cut anyone slack."

"Yeah." She chuckled. "I remember."

"Thanks for sharing my news about the bar, Mom."

"You're welcome, darlin'. Now, go give that man hell. You deserve the best, baby girl. Don't deny yourself that."

"I love you, Mama."

"I love you, too."

We hung up, and I went back to the dress. I picked it up and held it in my fingers as if I were holding something horrid. It was almost as if I were scared the dress would burn or scar me. Not that it would, but I couldn't help myself. I went back to my room with the dress in hand and opened my closet door. A full-length mirror was on the inside. I stood in front of it and held my breath.

The dress was stunning. It had lines of sequins that ran from the top of the waist to the bottom of the dress. I'd missed that when I first looked at it. Maybe it was the light in the room that picked it up, but whatever it was, the dress was beautiful.

And it was Prada. Between the shoes and the dress, this had to put Chase back quite a bit. For a charity. Almost contradictory to the entire purpose of the gala, but all proceeds went to the charity. So there was that.

Tomorrow was Monday, and I had to report to the office. The ball was next weekend. Would I still go with Chase? Right now I wasn't sure, but I did want to be there, to show my face, to prove to Patricia she was the piece of shit she was.

No amount of *I caught you fucking your boss* would keep me down. Hell to the fucking no!

I also needed to decide what I wanted to do with my future. Did I want to remain at his office and continue to see him day in and day out? Or did I want to move to a new office and start over? As much as I wanted to remain with his firm, it was a better solution to go with the latter.

I knew the decision I needed to make. I hung the dress in my closet and stared at it for a long moment. "You're so beautiful," I whispered with a smile. I touched it once more and then closed the closet door.

Back at my computer, I opened a new Word file and began the next note I would hand Chase Newstrom.

Dear Mr. Newstrom:

Consider this my resignation and two weeks' notice.

CHAPTER SIXTEEN

CHASE

It was a quarter to seven in the morning, with a crisp autumn breeze. If I weren't drenched in sweat, it wouldn't be so bad. Making my way up the elevator, my plan was to shower, get dressed, and be ready to take on the fight of my career: Ainsley.

When the elevator came to a stop and opened, however, the office lights were already on. Someone was present and accounted for. My stomach dropped, and nerves spiked in my chest with the pain of adrenaline.

I took the few steps toward the front door and gave it a tug. The receptionist wasn't there, but in the distance, I heard typing. I followed the sound, and when I turned the corner, she was there.

With a deep breath, I approached, unnerved... or the best I could muster. My gym towel was still around my neck, sitting atop my fitted tank and loose shorts.

She had her hair pulled into a messy bun, the auburn tendrils hanging loosely around her neckline. A white blouse was pulled almost taut to her body and paired with a black skirt.

A few more steps and I would pass her on the way to my office, my salvation.

"Mr. Newstrom," Ainsley called just as I stepped by her desk.

I paused and turned to face her. "No one else is here yet. Are we really going to do this?"

"Oh, like how you were just going to pass me toward your office as if I didn't exist?"

I raised a brow and crossed my arms over my chest. I noticed her eyes quickly move from mine to my chest and back. If I'd blinked, I would have missed it. Curious, I took a step toward her desk.

"Why are you here so early?"

She stood and fisted her hands by her side. "None of your business." She didn't try to hide the fact that she was definitely giving me the once-over.

If we hadn't had our falling out, I would have invited her to my office for "coffee" and to discuss what her duties would be today.

Blowjob.

Sex.

More sex.

But right now, I needed to keep my pants on. Ainsley turned away from me and headed toward the front of the office, and I couldn't help but watch her ass every step of the way.

When she reached the printer, she side-glanced me. I cleared my throat and headed toward my office. Once inside, I shut the door and leaned against it. We were the only ones here and only a few feet separated us; however, it felt like miles.

Her heels struck the tile as she made her way back to her desk. I peeked out the blinds in my office in time to see Ainsley take a seat at her desk. My chest tightened, and my stomach churned in knots.

I needed a shower. If I didn't watch myself, I would end

up hugging the porcelain throne.

◆ ◆ ◆ ◆

I worked my tie into a Windsor knot and set it with my diamond pin. I slicked my hair back and styled it with a little hair gel and then washed my hands. The day was still young—in fact, when I looked at the clock, it was still only eight a.m.—but there was much to do.

New cases.

Message the Vanderbilt family.

Discuss a countersuit against Miranda Cooper.

Order in lunch for my staff. I usually did this when we won a case.

Grovel at Ainsley's feet.

I took a seat at my desk and opened my email. There were a few new cases that had been brought to my firm that I needed to review. If they were potential clients, meetings would be set up, and that would include Ainsley's presence.

How the fuck would I meet with clients when the woman I was falling in love with sat next to me or across the table?

With a groan, I opened the first file and began to read, when a knock sounded at my door.

"Come in," I announced, and when I looked up, it was Ainsley. My heart sped and I jumped quickly to my feet, clenching and releasing my jaw a few times.

Was she here to talk about us? I had no idea.

"Ainsley?" I asked and came from around my desk.

She held a piece of paper in her hands. She closed the door behind her and lowered her gaze to the floor. "Mr. Newstrom, we need to talk."

"Don't do that," I said and took a few steps toward her. "After everything we've been through—"

"I passed my bar exam."

"I'm very happy for you!"

She bit her bottom lip and dug her left toe into the floor.

There was no reason for her to come in here and announce this unless we were good, right? I wanted to pull her into a hug. Maybe even spin her around a few times. But I was getting the sense we were not that couple anymore and the hugging would not be happening.

"Ainsley?"

She sighed and raised her eyes to meet mine. "I'm putting in my notice."

It felt like someone opened a wind tunnel, and the air hit my chest with such force, it nearly knocked me back on my ass.

"What?"

She crossed the room to where I stood, and with each step, the air grew thinner and thinner. I couldn't breathe. I couldn't move. I couldn't speak.

Ainsley reached out her hand that held the piece of paper she'd come in with.

I couldn't take it. This was not happening.

"Mr. Newstrom, I'm putting in my two weeks' notice," she repeated.

"No," I whispered. My chest wanted to cave in and explode in a fury of rage, but I only stood in silence.

She sighed and walked around me. I watched her move as she passed by and laid the paper on my desk. She turned to leave, so I reached for her and grabbed her arm.

"Let me go," she said in a soft voice. "Don't do this."

"Don't do what?" I asked. "Let you walk out of my life just

as I'm beginning to live for once?"

"This isn't about you," she said and turned to face me. "You always make it about you. Can you, for once, see things from my point of view?"

"I'm trying, but you need to give me time. Patience, please, Ainsley."

"Patience for what? So you can get your dick sucked anytime you want from me? No, Chase. That's not the career I signed up for when I agreed to protect and enforce the law. I'm leaving so I can start my career on a good note in an office that has no idea who I am. And I'll need you to give me a good letter of recommendation. It's the least you could do after making it plainly obvious to your ex that I'd had sex with you—my boss."

I let her arm go. Her words stung like a wasp... No, like a hot sword slicing through my frozen heart. I needed her in my life, and I couldn't let her walk out that door.

I had two weeks.

Two weeks was enough to make a huge impact. It would allow me the time to show her I was more than a womanizing manwhore who used and left women at the curb. How the hell I would do this, I didn't know.

"Please," I started and took a few steps toward her. "Don't leave. Not like this."

"Why do you need me here?" she asked.

Silence filled the space between us.

"Is it for your next case? Fine. I'll help you while I can, but once my time is up, I'm gone." She turned toward the door a second time.

The air was being sucked from my lungs again. I wanted to drop to my knees and beg her not to go. I'd never been one to beg. Hell, I'd never had to. Anything and everything I'd ever wanted was always given to me.

And that was my problem. I was losing something I could not have.

"Ainsley," I called out once more as she reached the door. She paused but didn't look my way.

"Did you get the dress?" I was hoping, praying, this would make her turn around. Even if it were anger at the gesture of sending her a garment and shoes, I would take it just to keep her here a moment longer.

Who the hell had I become? Was this what Brice was talking about with love? I hated this feeling more than anything in the world, but in the same breath, I couldn't have a life without Ainsley being a part of it.

She turned on her heel and faced me full-on. "Yes, I did. And the shoes."

I smiled, and it felt like I had won a small battle of this war between us. "I'm glad."

"It doesn't mean I'm going to wear it to the ball, though," she added. "I don't know if I'm still going."

And like that, my battle was lost . . . except for the small hole in her story.

I don't know if I'm still going.

I could work with that. I could hold on to that piece of material and make it work in my favor.

"Then I'll send Andrew by to pick you up."

"I just said I don't know if I'm going," she said and crossed her arms over her chest.

"I understand that, but if there's a chance you may want to go, Andrew will be there to bring you." I sucked in air and took a chance. I crossed the room to where she stood. I looked down into her eyes and reached toward her.

She shook her head and took a step back. "Please, don't do that."

"Why not?"

"Because if you do, I may not be able to stop myself," she whispered.

Hope rose, and I took it full force with a step forward into her space. "Ainsley," I whispered. "I need you in my life."

"Chase, stop, please," she said, and dampness glistened in her eyes.

"Why? I want you, Ainsley. I need you with me. I never knew how much until I no longer had you. Please, don't go." I meant every word. I wanted to pull her to me, hold her body against mine, kiss every inch of her, and make love to her until we could no longer move.

"Because I need someone to support me, respect me, and keep people like Patricia out of my business," Ainsley said. "Because of what she witnessed, she could ruin any chance I have at this career. How do you not see that?"

"Because she's a fucking tramp, and no one takes anything she says seriously." Anger rose in my words, but not toward Ainsley. The rage was all for Patricia. I hated her and the time I would never get back that was spent with her. How the hell did I ever think I could love such a demon of a woman?

"And you fucked her, just like you fucked me. So how does that make me look in your colleagues' eyes?"

"I could give a fuck what they think," I said, my voice raised. "You. Are. Not. Patricia!"

"Well thank fuck for that!"

Ainsley sidestepped me and headed toward my door. I couldn't let her leave. Not now. We were finally getting somewhere, and damn it, she was mine. I reached for her once more, and with a pull, I yanked her back to me. Her body slammed into mine, and I pushed her up against the wall.

"What the hell do you think you're doing?" she yelled.

"Everything and nothing. Right now, tell me what you want, Ainsley. Tell me you want me and want this thing between us to work out. Tell me you want it as much as I do. Tell me I'm not the crazy one in thinking you're my soul mate. Tell me, please . . . for the love of all things holy, woman, tell me!"

She stared into my eyes for a moment and didn't say anything. I was confessing my love for her without saying the three words she wanted to hear most. And the asshole I was, I couldn't do it. I couldn't say it. Even if those three words were to save her life.

"I shouldn't have to tell you that, Chase. That's just it." She placed her hands on my chest but didn't push me away. Instead, she brought them to my cheeks and cupped my face. "If I hadn't drunk your Scotch and written you that letter, would we even be standing right here, right now?"

I wanted more than anything to lean into her, press my lips against hers, and never let go. But a kiss would not answer the one question that hung between us.

What if that never happened?

With a sigh, I took hold of her wrists. My heart shattered into pieces as I pulled her hands from me and took a few steps back. I lowered my gaze to the floor and shook my head.

"I . . . I don't know."

She sniffed, and when she spoke, she had tears in her voice. "And that's why I need to leave. Goodbye, Chase."

And a little piece of me died.

Ainsley sidestepped me once more, and this time I didn't

stop her. I heard the door open and close with a gentle click. The air in the room suddenly engulfed me and brought me to my knees.

What the fuck had I just done?

CHAPTER SEVENTEEN

AINSLEY

The dress hung before me like a bomb ready to explode. My mind ticked like a stopwatch. It was only a matter of time before the ticking stopped and something tremendous happened. I could have the night of my life with the man of my dreams, or the night could end on a sour note and I would go on to die an old cat lady.

My stomach clenched, and I felt thankful I hadn't eaten anything. It would have surely ended up on the floor in front of me. I nibbled on my bottom lip and stood naked in front of the red satin dress. I wanted to reach out and touch it, but feeling it made it real, and I wasn't sure I was ready for that. At least not yet…

"Ainsley, you back there?" Everly, my sister, called.

I breathed a sigh of relief. She was here. I had called her earlier, frantic, about tonight. I needed someone to prep me for this event, and who better than my stylist sister? She stepped into my white-walled bedroom, which was decorated with a few pictures of legal libraries and knickknack items I'd collected.

"I'm back here," I called. "Warning… I'm naked."

I heard Everly chuckle. "Won't be the first time seeing you in the buff." She crossed the threshold of my bedroom and lifted a brow. "Wow, sis, you look like shit."

I crossed my arms over my chest with a huff. "Well, thank you so much. That's why you're here—so I won't look like shit." I rolled my eyes and motioned to the dress. "Here's what you're working with. What can you do?"

Everly smiled, turned toward the dress, and gasped. "Holy fuck nuggets, is that a Prada?" She approached it and lifted her hand to the fabric but didn't touch it. She let her hand hover over the material, and her breath shuddered.

"What is wrong with you?" I asked, amused. I turned toward my bed and sat down on my dark-blue comforter. I pulled up the side and wrapped it around my body. "It's just a dress."

"No," she whispered. "Don't listen to her. She didn't mean it, baby. You're so beautiful."

I shook my head and gave my sister a moment of lovemaking with the dress. "When you're done having your orgasmic material moment, I need you to do my hair, makeup, and get me in this dress."

"Shoes" was all Everly said.

"What?"

"Shoes. There have to be shoes to go with this magnificent dress. Where are they?"

I snickered to myself and laid my fingers over my lips for a moment. "I'd show you, but I'm afraid you'll try to kiss and lick them."

She glared over her shoulder at me and then rolled her eyes as she went back to the dress. "Don't worry, baby. Auntie Everly loves you."

"You're so strange," I told her. Honestly, I'd needed this distraction. My stomach no longer felt nauseated, although thinking of the ball set the rumblings on overdrive. "Everly, I'm scared."

This got her attention. She turned around and made her way over to my bed. "Which part? Wearing the dress in front of all the people you don't know, or wearing the dress Chase sent you in front of all the people you don't know?"

I sighed and looked at my hands. I fidgeted with my fingers and picked at my nail. "I'm scared of him and how I feel about him."

She slapped at my hands and tsked at me to not pick my fingers. "Go with your head held high and own that place. They don't own you. Hell, they don't know you. So go in there and own it, Ainsley. Hold on to Chase's arm if you need to, but be your own woman. You've got this, sister. Now, if you're good to get ready, I'll doll you up and cry while I put this beauty on your ungrateful body."

"Seriously, you're weird." I then pulled my sister into a hug. "Thank you," I whispered. "You always know just what to say."

She hugged me back. "You're welcome. Trust me, you'll know what to do when the time comes." She pulled back and cupped my face. "If that means confessing your love for Chase Newstrom, do it. If it means giving him up and walking away"—she lowered her hands to her lap—"I'll be here with Ben & Jerry's for our evening consumption."

I nodded and felt dampness jet down my cheek. I quickly swiped it away. "Thank you again."

"Right. Let's get you dressed!"

♦ ♦ ♦ ♦

"Turn," Everly told me. "Let me see you in full action."

I felt like a princess. My hair was pulled into an upsweep, with a few tendrils around my face, the dress fit me perfectly, and the shoes—the shoes would make me change my stance on fashion. These shoes were quite amazing. I felt like Julia Roberts in *Pretty Woman*. Well, except for the gazillion-dollar necklace.

Everly opened her purse and pulled out a string of pearls. I gasped when I saw them.

"Those were our grandmother's!"

"Yes," she said. "And tonight, they're yours. Now turn around."

She lifted the necklace over my head, and the chilled pearls lay against my chest. They hung just below my neckline, and in the center was a round platinum band with a row of diamonds. I reached up and touched it with my fingertips. I could remember our grandmother wearing this on special occasions. The scent of her perfume invaded my mind, and it was as if she were here with me.

"I have some diamond earrings," I announced in the silence. "You think they'll be okay?"

"Are they studs?"

I nodded.

"Then yes, they'll be perfect."

I went to my bathroom and opened my wooden jewelry box. It was something my father had given me when I was a child. I'd had it for as long as I can remember and still used it to this day. I loved it in a sentimental way. I found my diamonds and pulled them out. When I looked up to the mirror, I paused and simply stared at myself.

My makeup was perfectly airbrushed, the shadows were

on point, and my lipstick was the color of my dress. My eyes watered at the image in the mirror. This wasn't me, was it? Maybe I *was* Julia Roberts going to the royal ball after all.

"Are you okay?" I heard Everly ask.

"Yes, I'm okay. I hadn't seen myself yet." I let go of a long breath and then slid my earrings into place. I turned to face my waiting sister and held my arms out. "Well?"

She smiled. "Absolute perfection."

My doorbell rang, and my stomach fluttered, knotted, and I felt sick all at once. "What do I do?" I whispered.

She smiled and, with a wink, said, "You go own that ass, sister. You show him who's in charge and make the night yours." She left my bedroom and headed to what I assumed was my front door.

I grabbed the small black pearl clutch I'd picked up in a boutique the other day and slipped my lipstick, license, and keys inside. With a deep breath, I walked out of my bedroom and headed down the short distance to my living room and entrance.

When I stepped into the room, Chase and Everly both looked at me. He stood in a tuxedo, with a bowtie that matched the color of my dress. His hair was styled perfectly. Even his shoes were perfect.

I paused, hesitating to move forward until Everly smiled. She winked at me, and I felt a smile slowly creep across my lips as I stepped into the living room.

Chase took a step toward me, and his eyes—his beautiful blue eyes—were wide with wonder. He looked at me with adoration, longing and, if I wasn't mistaken, love. It made my heart skip a beat and my feet want to run toward him.

But I didn't. I stood my ground, mainly because I was

afraid I'd trip. My legs were weak, whereas a moment ago I was just fine. This man...this incredible, beautiful man. I was in love with him, and there was no going back.

"Ainsley," he whispered. "You are absolutely stunning." He reached out his hand, and I rested mine in his. He brought it to his lips and placed a soft kiss on the back of it.

I smiled. "Thank you." I felt a blush rush up my neck and cheeks. "You look quite handsome yourself."

"Shall we?" he asked.

I nodded. "We shall."

Everything from his office, my pushing him away, and Patricia walking in on us... It all disappeared. I wanted to hold on to tonight as my dream, but I knew soon reality would hit. We would enter the gala, and the facade would fade. He would mingle with his lawyer friends, and I would find those I knew.

Then there was Patricia. She would be there. What would I do when she approached me? A woman who walked with confidence would not need to size up her competition, but that wasn't Patricia. She was a predator readying herself to pounce on her prey, and tonight, that would be me.

What would Chase do in this situation? Would he take my side and tell Patricia to fuck off? Would he stay with his friends and watch the event unfold? My heart knew he would do the former, but my mind screamed the latter.

He tucked my hand under his arm and turned to my sister. "I'll have her home later tonight."

She snorted and motioned toward the door. "Don't bother telling me that. I have my own place. This is hers. As long as she survives the night, get her home on your own time."

"Everly," I groaned.

She giggled and opened the door. "Have fun, you two!" She walked out and left the door open in her wake.

I looked up at Chase. "Well, are you ready?"

"I would rather stay here and admire you in this dress. Then devour you out of it."

As amazing as that sounded right now—and it did—we needed to make an appearance. I also needed time to talk to him about me . . . about us.

"Maybe after the party."

He lifted his brows. "Well, let's go, then."

Moments later, we were driving down the boulevard toward Rosewood Mansion in Dallas. This was one of the most beautiful hotels in the city, and I'd never been inside. The car ride was quiet except for soft music that played through the cab. The driver's partition window was rolled up for privacy.

I glanced over at Chase and found him fiddling with his fingers in his lap. Was he nervous? Anxious?

My heart hurt from the experience at his home when Patricia had walked in. I'd felt completely exposed. Was that his fault? No, not necessarily, but I wasn't ready for anyone to know we were an item, assuming we even were that.

But my heart also ached for him in a way I had never felt. I wanted him in my life. It was so much more than sex. It was love. I knew it, and I would wager he knew it as well.

I reached for his hand and slipped mine into it. His palm was clammy, definitely nervous. He looked at me, and I smiled. "Are you all right?"

He nodded. "Yeah, I'm good." He sighed. "No, I'm not. I lied. I'm sorry. I'm not all right. My head hurts, and I want to turn this car around and head back to your place and never come out again."

I smiled again at his words. I wanted to tell him how I felt. To yell to the skies that I loved Chase Newstrom and would give anything to be with him. I wanted to tell him everything and show him exactly how I felt about him in my bed.

"Chase," I started but was cut off by his driver.

"We'll be there in five minutes, sir. Do you wish to be dropped off at the front or near the back?"

Chase looked at me and raised his brows. "What would you prefer?"

"The front. I honestly don't care."

"The front," he repeated to the driver.

"Very well," he said, and silence once again enveloped us.

Chase cleared his throat and looked at me again. "You were saying?"

I sighed and pulled my hand from his. "We're almost there. Another time, maybe."

"No, go ahead. What were you going to say?" He took my hand back into his and placed his other hand on top, covering mine completely.

They were warm, and I briefly recalled how they felt on my body. I shivered. I opened my mouth to tell him everything, but we came to a stop.

Flashes erupted through the window, and the door to our car was opened. Cameras were shoved inside, and flash after flash went off. A hand was extended for me, and I looked at Chase. He simply smiled.

"Go on. We'll talk later. I promise," he said.

I nodded, and with a sigh of defeat, I held one hand in front of my face to block the bright lights of the cameras and accepted the extended hand with my other. I stood from the car, and warm air surrounded my body. Exhaust, too much perfume, and cigarette smoke filled the air. I coughed and held on to the hand that helped me out. It was his driver, Andrew.

"Don't let me fall," I told him.

He smiled and patted my hand. "Never."

"I'll take her from here," Chase spoke and took my hand in his.

I looked at him and felt ease settle over me. Soon we would be inside and out of the flashes, yells, and polluted air.

"Why are the paparazzi here?" I asked.

"This is one of the biggest events of the year in our area. Law firms aren't the only ones who support this cause. There are some wealthy investors, professional athletes, and celebrities as well."

I nodded as we walked up the steps toward the gala. I wasn't sure what to expect, and even with the animosity behind us, for the most part, Chase was my home base tonight. And if I needed a quick out, I had my sister or Uber.

Let the festivities begin.

CHAPTER EIGHTEEN

CHASE

If someone had told me a month ago that my date for tonight's event would be Ainsley Speire, I would have called them a liar. But here we were.

I looked at her and smiled as she took in our environment. She was stunning. Exquisite. I wanted to take her away from here and do naughty things with her. All in due time— assuming, of course, our fighting spell was behind us.

We walked into the ball. A large glass sculpture of a mermaid sat atop a mound of rocks, and the water that was her backdrop was formed of ice. It was striking.

Some of the wealthiest people from Dallas and the surrounding areas were here tonight. Money was thrown around in ways that was almost sickening. So many had so little, while we were going to eat off five-thousand-dollars-per-plate settings. I wasn't sure I'd actually cared about that small detail before tonight. That was also, of course, before Ainsley.

How I hadn't really seen Ainsley before she wrote her note would always be beyond me. I should thank her again tonight for getting drunk and letting her feelings flow. I smirked to myself as we walked farther into the gala.

From tuxedos to expensive ball gowns, no one had spared

any pennies. I wondered, since we were putting on a charity event, if the dress attire should have been T-shirt and jeans rather than million-dollar outfits. Seemed to be a complete oxymoron.

"What's on your mind?" Ainsley asked me.

I gave a slight shrug. "I guess I'm actually wondering why we're really here tonight."

She raised her brows. "Meaning?"

A waiter approached with a silver tray and eight flutes of champagne. I took two and handed one to Ainsley.

"Meaning this," I said and held my goblet up to clink hers. I took a sip before continuing. "All this money spent preparing and putting on this charity ball, where said charity would see none of it."

She nodded in understanding. "So you're saying invest all this money that funded this ball into the charity itself?"

"Yep, exactly."

"I couldn't have said it better myself." She took another sip and then winked at me.

I chuckled and pulled her just slightly closer. "Does this mean you forgive me?"

A slight blush colored her neck and touched her cheeks. She grinned a coy smile and lowered her gaze to the floor. "Maybe," she whispered. "We'll see where we are after tonight, okay?"

She looked up and had a twinkle of mischief in her eyes, and I knew groveling—as well as her naked body—would be in my future. And I couldn't wait to get started.

"Sounds perfect," I told her. Movement across the room caught my attention, and when I looked up, it was the mayor of Dallas. "Give me a minute, would you? I'm being summoned.

Are you okay to mingle alone?"

She nibbled on her lip for a moment and looked to her left and then her right. She squared her shoulders and gave a curt nod. "I'll be fine."

"That's my girl," I whispered and feathered a kiss on her cheek, just next to her ear.

"Mr. Newstrom," she said and held on to my arm. "If we're to be associates at work, it wouldn't be wise to kiss me so openly."

I grinned, and while I was still next to her ear, I cupped my mouth around it and whispered, "If I wanted to be open with you in front of everyone, my lips would be on your body and not your cheek."

I could feel Ainsley shiver at my words as my breath fanned across her ear.

I leaned back and raised my brow. I met her gaze, and her face flushed with a new level of arousal. I hoped the growing erection in my pants would not give me away when I left her side, but a good adjustment wouldn't warrant any second glances.

"You drive me crazy, woman," I told her with a wink.

She giggled and took a sip of her champagne. "I do what I can."

I grinned and kissed the top of her hand and then let her go as I made my way toward the mayor.

The man was tall, clean-shaven, and had a head full of silver hair. His tuxedo was topped off with a red bowtie. He smiled and held out his right hand.

I took it with a firm shake. "Mayor Martin," I said.

"Mr. Newstrom, it's been a while. Are you ready to switch sides yet and fight for the justice of our victims?"

I chuckled and let his hand go. "No, sir. I'll continue to fight for the true victims."

The district attorney approached with a smirk. He was tall and slender in build, which only drew more attention to his long, polka-dotted tie. It was an odd ensemble, but so was the DA. He was quite a character and enjoyed telling the occasional joke. He'd told me once that enemies could be brought together when a chuckle could be shared.

"Chase," he started and held his hand out.

I took it. "Brian." After we shook, the DA shoved his hand into his pants pockets. "Are you looking to switch sides? The election isn't up yet, and I have no plans on leaving my spot."

I laughed and shook my head. "No, you're good. No worries there. How's your wife, Amelia?"

"She's fine. Thanks for asking."

"Well, if it isn't a few of my favorite men!"

I heard the shrill of a familiar voice and gritted my teeth. The three of us turned to find Patricia headed our direction. A part of me was relieved she hadn't targeted Ainsley, but the other part was now on guard for whatever poison she planned to release into the wild tonight.

"Patricia," the mayor said and pulled her in for a hug. "It's been a while since I've heard your name. How're things going?"

"Good, Mayor Martin."

"Please, just James," he said.

She nodded and turned to Brian. She pulled him in for a hug and kissed his cheek, leaving a red splotch. He met my gaze, and I smiled and held my champagne glass up for a cheer. I didn't plan to tell him there was lipstick on his cheek.

"And that leaves me with Chase," she said with a rude

tone. She placed her hands on her hips and lifted a brow. "Are you still fucking your intern?"

"Excuse me?" I asked and bit back the rage that threatened to explode.

"That's a large accusation there," the mayor said in a lowered tone. "And I would suggest this isn't the setting for language like that."

"Oh, no problem, sir," Patricia started, "but the woman who has been interning for him was found riding him pretty hard. I mean, if she wants to fuck her way to the top, who am I to stop her?"

"I'm sorry, but did I just hear you right?" said a voice behind me.

My heart skipped a beat when I turned to find Ainsley on a quick approach.

"Shit," I whispered.

Patricia crossed her arms over her chest and held her chin high. "Yes, you did. I mean, I never had to sleep my way to the top, but you do you, honey."

I sighed and closed my eyes. *How the fuck can this be happening?* I ran my hand through my styled hair and looked at the mayor. "I'm so sorry, sir. Please excuse us. We'll be going now."

"No, you don't need to leave," the mayor said. He turned to Patricia. "You, Patricia, can see yourself out. We don't need someone like you polluting our environment with your hatred."

She held her hands up in mock surrender. "I was only saying, Mayor, that if you want people like Ainsley Speire representing victims and criminals while fucking them at the same time, who am I to stop you?"

Ainsley shook her head.

I couldn't even imagine the rage she felt at this moment.

"You're unbelievable," Ainsley told her. "You walked in on an innocent situation and twisted it for your own amusement. How is it possible that you've ever won a case?"

That caught me by surprise. Even the mayor and DA chuckled.

Ainsley did a double-take at the DA and pointed to his cheek. "You might want to get that off. There's a bit of skank on your cheek."

I laughed and then coughed to cover it.

Patricia huffed, her face growing redder the longer she stood with us. "Well, everyone knows Chase sleeps with anything with a fucking hole."

"I slept with you," I whispered.

"Me too, though it was a long time ago, before I was married," the DA announced.

We all looked to the mayor, and he held his hands up. "Hell no. I wouldn't touch that."

Patricia growled and started toward Ainsley.

I stepped in front of my lady and shook my head. "Don't you even think about it. You had a lot of nerve showing up unannounced at my home, and now you're accusing Ainsley of sleeping with her boss? You realize that is slander, right?"

She huffed once more and opened her mouth to say something, when Ainsley tugged at my arm. I stepped to the side as she stepped around me. She was now the predator, and Patricia was her prey. Even the mayor and DA took a step back in her presence.

"Right," Ainsley started. "And you're now jealous he didn't want to sleep with you once he realized you were simply after his money. He even walked in on you with his best friend." She shook her head and clucked her tongue. "But hey, that's none of my business." Ainsley then took a sip of her champagne.

Patricia's mouth hung open in shocked horror. No one had ever talked to her this way, as far as I knew. Her hands fisted by her sides.

I slid my arm around Ainsley's waist. "Well, if there's nothing else," I offered and tugged Ainsley into my side. "You were told to leave." Like Ainsley, I took a sip of my champagne.

Patricia looked to the mayor and then to the DA. Neither man would meet her eyes. She growled, turned around with a scream, and stalked out of our range. The DA reached up with a napkin and began to wipe at his cheek. He shook his head with a chuckle.

"I have never witnessed anything quite like that before. Don't let her get away," he said and motioned to Ainsley.

I smiled. "I don't plan on it. By the way, she just passed the bar."

"Congratulations," the DA told her. "If you ever want to come play for the other team, my door will always be open."

"Thank you, sir. That's quite generous."

He shook her hand and made his exit.

"Well, I guess that was our entertainment for the evening," the mayor said. He shook my hand once more and then offered his hand to Ainsley. She took it and smiled. "I'm sorry about all that, and congratulations."

She waved it off. "Don't worry about it, and thank you." Ainsley sipped her champagne and then set the empty glass on a silver tray as a waiter walked by.

Someone tapped the microphone in the room, and our

attention turned to the stage. The master of ceremonies was about to give a speech.

I looked at Ainsley and tucked a few strands of hair behind her ear. "Are you all right?"

She nodded with a smile. "Perfect. I need to get used to dealing with people like Patricia."

I smiled and ran a gentle finger over her cheek. "Good, I'm glad. Because if you're going to continue to work for me, we need to lay some ground rules."

Something naughty glinted in her eyes as she spoke. "I want my corner office to have an amazing view of the city."

I raised my brows. "Woman, you must first pay your dues to get a view like that."

She shrugged. "Then I'll move into your office, and you can figure out where to go."

I laughed and shook my head. "I need to go make my speech here shortly. Don't do anything reckless." I tilted her head up slightly and smiled.

"If you kiss me in front of everyone, it'll be a scandal," she teased.

"I don't care who knows," I said and slanted my lips over hers. My chest ached from the beating of my heart. My blood rushed through my body and heated me in places that should be reserved for later. I held her in my arms for a long moment, and she whimpered against my mouth. When I released her from the kiss, I pressed my forehead to hers.

"I'm falling in love with you, Ainsley Speire."

"Will Chase Newstrom please come join me on stage?" the emcee announced.

I feathered a kiss to her forehead. "I'll be right back." I met her gaze. Her eyes were damp with tears, but her smile could have warmed my heart for the rest of my days.

CHAPTER NINETEEN

AINSLEY

I'd never believed a woman could be swept off her feet, but Chase just managed to do it to me. My knees felt weak when he told me he was falling in love. Hell, I'd already fallen. He took the steps toward the stage, shook the emcee's hand, and then turned to the microphone.

Chase was meant for this. He came alive up on the stage. His eyes lit up, and he smiled as he talked. He explained why we were here today and talked about the charity. His words came as naturally to him as breaths did. I couldn't help but smile at the man on stage.

My man.

My Chase.

"When I was younger, I went on a date with a girl I knew in high school," he spoke into the microphone. "I think I was seventeen. I already knew I wanted to be a lawyer, but I wasn't quite sure what part of the law I wanted to study. When I went on the date with this girl, she was a year younger than me. She wasn't sure what she wanted to be, which was probably ninety percent of my graduating class."

The audience chuckled in appreciation and understanding.

I thought back to my high school days. I always knew I

wanted to be an attorney.

"After our date, I took her home and wished her good night. The next day, while I was in class, the police came in and escorted me out. My mind raced with worst-case scenarios."

Chase began to count on his fingers.

"My father died. My mother was in the hospital. Something had happened to my brother. But no. It wasn't anything like that." He paused for a moment and met my gaze. I smiled, and he held his gaze for just a moment, and then he winked at me. "They were there for me."

There was a subtle gasp across the audience. Chase kept his private life private. So why share now?

"I had been accused of raping the girl I went on that date with."

More gasps. I took another glass of champagne from a waiter who was passing by and sipped it.

There was murmuring through the audience, and a few looked my way.

I smiled and motioned for their attention to be on Chase. I knew the truth and wholeheartedly believed him.

"I was arrested and brought to a juvenile detention center. My mom hired an attorney to fight for me, but it wasn't until later that the DA learned the girl had made up her story."

I glanced over to the district attorney of Dallas and found him smiling up at Chase. I returned my attention to the beautiful man on stage as he continued his speech.

"Like my last case with Lance Vanderbilt. One simple rumor can ruin a person's entire future. And this was why I decided to become a defense attorney. To help those who need help. I'll do that now by donating all fees received from the Vanderbilt case to tonight's fundraiser."

The audience clapped again, followed by a few hoots and hollers.

My eyes filled with tears, and my heart swelled with more love than I thought possible. He wanted to do so much for so many others, and they would never know who it came from. Chase Newstrom was so much more of a man than anyone else I had ever met.

And I loved him.

I smiled at the affirmation, and a part of me wanted to jump up and down and scream it to the skies that I loved Chase Newstrom. Although if I did, I would look like a lunatic, so said screaming would have to wait for tonight.

After the applause died down, Chase continued his speech. "I'll have everyone here know I won the Vanderbilt case because of the hard work of a very special woman. Miss Ainsley Speire joined my team just after she took her bar exam. And I'll have you know she passed!"

More applause sounded, and my cheeks got so hot, I thought I would combust in flames. The few who were standing by us when he kissed me turned in my direction. There was a good chance they'd also heard the conversation with Patricia, but I honestly didn't care. Let them think what they wanted. I loved Chase Newstrom, and if I wasn't mistaken, he essentially confessed his love for me tonight as well.

"You know, she was so pissed off at me during the trial, she got into my best Scotch and drank the entire contents."

"Oh, hell," I whispered and held my hand over my eyes. "Please, no. Just no."

"She wrote me the ugliest note, telling me to basically go eff... erm, go screw myself."

The audience members chuckled, and I peeked at him through my fingers.

"She also said a few choice things of a different nature that I'll leave to your imagination."

A few whistles and catcalls sounded, and I had never wanted a room to open up and swallow me whole more desperately than right now.

"Get 'er," someone yelled out.

Chase held his hand up and shook a single finger. "It's not like that, but I have to say, the woman opened my eyes that day. It was then that working with Ainsley became a game-changer. She helped me win that case. And throughout our time together, I have managed to fall in love with her—the one woman who was able to melt my ice-cold heart. The world better get ready for Ainsley Speire. She's going to be one hell of an attorney." He pointed to the DA with a grin. "You'd better be ready for the fight of your life!"

"Bring it!" the DA yelled with a smile.

Chase brought the mic up once more. Lord, was he going to wrap up soon? Hell, no more secrets or information about me, please.

"Even though I'm not involved with cases of battered women and children, that would never stop me and my firm from donating to this amazing foundation. Thank you for being here tonight, enjoy yourselves, and let your wallets flow freely!"

The audience clapped for Chase as he exited the stage, and a few hands reached to shake his.

I stood off to the side and allowed him to have his moment. He was a brilliant man, but maybe someone should write his speeches for him.

He pushed through the crowd and came back to my side with a larger-than-life smile on his lips. I could have melted into him, right there, with the way he looked at me. He was everything, and right now I was his world.

"Now everyone knows I belong to you, baby," he said just to me.

"You had nothing to prove up there," I told him and slipped my arms around his neck.

"I know, but I wanted the world to know my heart belonged to you and you alone."

His words melted me even more.

"The world, huh?"

He nodded and rested his forehead against mine. "I want to take you home and make love to your sweet body and do things to you I've been dying to try."

"Oh, I'm curious. What do you have in mind?"

He grinned. "Curious kitten, my speech is over and my check has been delivered. We can go whenever you'd like."

My pussy clenched with need, and I wanted more than anything to feel Chase between my legs, pushing himself deep inside, claiming me as his.

"Oh, I don't know. I'm kinda hungry. I wanted to meet a few more of the city officials, you know, really get my name out there as this kick-ass attorney."

He grinned, and it was so beautiful. I wanted to frame this moment in my memory forever.

"I should begin introducing you as Criminal Attorney Miss Ainsley Speire."

I loved the sound of that. I smiled so hard, it hurt my cheeks. "Whoever said I wanted to be a criminal attorney?"

His brows rose. "You did?"

The look of questionable integrity caused me to laugh. He looked scared and also confused at the same time. "Oh, stop. I'd love for you to introduce me that way."

He grinned and then waggled his brows. "So, shall we leave, then?"

I nodded. "Yes, let's get out of here."

In the darkness of his limo, Chase managed to get me onto his lap. I straddled his hips and cupped his face, our lips fighting for dominance as our tongues wrestled in a rhythmic dance of seduction. The partition window was up, separating us from Andrew.

"I need to be inside you, woman," he whispered.

"Then move my panties and touch me," I told him.

Chase didn't hesitate. He moved his hand down between us, and I lifted just enough to give him access to my delicates that separated me from his body ... Well, his pants. He was still dressed. So only one of us would be having fun at the moment.

With a wicked grin, Chase maneuvered his fingers past my panties and slid his digits over my wet pussy. He slid in two fingers and pumped them, filling me with only a tease of what would come later.

"I want to taste you on my tongue," he teased.

"Just get me naked before we ruin this dress. My sister wants to marry it."

He stopped what he was doing and laughed a hard chuckle. "Well that was random, but okay. We'll save the dress for her special occasion."

I tilted his head up and slanted my mouth across his. He pumped his fingers faster and rubbed the sensitive spot inside me. The friction drove me crazy, and a subtle hint of an orgasm teased. Hell, I needed him so much more than what his fingers could do for me.

I moved my hips in rhythm with his hand. My breaths came heavier and with a frantic need. I reached for his pants buckle.

"Wait, my love. Wait until we get back to your place," he begged. "Not here. You're worth so much more to me than a car fuck."

"Right. I'm a great car fuck as well as bed, wall, or anywhere else you take me."

He chuckled. "You're so bad, woman."

"You love it," I whispered and nibbled on his ear.

"That I do," he said and pressed his thumb to my clit. He moved it with aggression that met the rhythm of his fingers.

I gasped and sat back in his lap, giving him fuller access to my body. "Yes," I moaned and reached for the handle above the door of the car. I held on and moved my body with desperation against his hand. He moved his thumb faster, pushed his fingers harder, and my body would soon shatter.

"Chase," I said in a higher pitch. "Chase, oh, God."

"Hold on for me, baby. Hold on. We're almost there."

"Unless you stop, I won't be able to hold on. I'm going to come. Please, I need to. I've needed you, needed this."

Then, without warning, he stopped. He pulled his hand free from me.

I looked at him, confused and, honestly, pissed off. "What the hell, Chase?"

"I need you to wait, please. Don't let yourself go here in this car. You deserve to be cherished, not fucked."

I smiled and leaned into him. "But you're not fucking me.

Your fingers were, and they were doing a damn good job."

He chuckled. "Please, give me this, baby."

I sighed and collapsed against his chest, into his arms. "Fine," I groaned. "But as soon as we're in—"

"You're mine, baby."

I grinned and buried my face into his neck, kissing his skin under his ear. "Thank you."

"For what?" he asked.

"For this amazing night. For being you. For standing up for me."

"If I recall, you stood up for yourself just fine."

I nodded and then looked at him. "Yes, but you were there and supported me rather than let that bitch walk all over me."

He brushed strands of loose hair back from my face. "I would never feed you to the wolves, baby."

I leaned into him once more and relished the feel of his arms around my body. He was my safety net, my man, my person. I had fallen in love with Chase Newstrom, the unclaimable man, the one who swore to have had an ice heart . . . and he was mine.

CHAPTER TWENTY

AINSLEY

If you had asked me a month or so ago if Chase Newstrom was "the one," I would have laughed and told you to fuck off. The man was a sex god, and his personality and attitude personified that fact. However, since I've come to know the man, after having shared intimate relations with him and handing my heart over completely, the answer would be a resounding *yes*. He was the one.

We left his car quickly, not wanting to break our momentum toward a much-needed, hard-as-you-can-fuck-me, just-got-over-the-biggest-fight-ever, you-belong-to-me-now fuck session. When we stood before the door of my building, Chase placed his hands over my breasts, pulling my back against his chest. He feathered his lips across my exposed neckline, and shivers ran up and down my spine.

"Open the fucking door already," he growled next to my ear. My body quaked with need as his tongue slid along my earlobe.

"I'm trying," I said with an exasperated sigh. "You're not making it easy on me."

He chuckled this dark, throaty sound that brought a grin to my lips. "Do you have any idea what do you to me?" Chase pressed his erection into the crease of my ass, and if his hardness was any indication, I knew exactly how I made him feel.

My key finally turned in the deadbolt, and the door shot open. We stumbled inside, and I managed to close the door behind me before Chase pressed my back to it.

His hands were on my breasts again, and his lips—his gorgeous, luscious mouth—claimed my own in a show of dominance. He pressed his knee between my thighs, and I moved my left leg around his thigh. He moved his hands from my chest long enough to gather the skirts of my dress and pull them up toward my waist.

"I need these clothes off your delicious body," he groaned against my lips.

"I can't get out of said clothes unless you let me go."

He grinned, and a soft laugh escaped him. "Not a chance."

"Then you'll have to make do with my clothes on," I teased. It took more willpower than I was willing to admit to keep myself from shoving his jacket off and ripping his shirt—and his pants—at the buttons.

He thrust his erection against my pussy, and the friction sent a jolt of adrenaline through my veins. I groaned in the silence of my home and fisted my hands atop his shoulders. My arms began to shake, and the one leg I stood on weakened. I wanted to shatter in his arms, give myself to him completely, but was he ready and willing to do the same?

The way he was with me at the event tonight, from his demeanor in front of watching eyes to the zero fucks given to those who watched him kiss me, told me everything I needed to know. A boldness I wasn't sure I had erupted from my inner self and took over, like turning on the autopilot of my body.

In a rushed frenzy, I grabbed at his jacket and pushed it

from his shoulders to his elbows. "Get naked," I growled and pushed it the rest of the way off his arms. I reached for and removed his bowtie and then tore his shirt's material from its buttons.

"Oops, I'm sorry," I whispered.

"Fuck the shirt," he growled and pushed my arms above my head. He held my wrists with one hand while the other took hold of my chin. "I'm going to ravish every inch of your body, Ainsley. Every fucking inch. Tell me you're mine. Tell me you belong to me." He leaned in, and his nose teased mine, followed by his tongue across my lips. I could feel his breath on my mouth as he spoke. "Tell me you love me, Ainsley."

My breath rushed from my lungs, and my legs gave out from under me. He wrapped his arm around my waist and held me against his body. *Tell me you love me. Tell me you're mine.* His words sang over and over in my head—the words I'd been wanting to hear, longing to hear, needing to hear for so long.

"I'm yours," I whispered. "Please, Chase, release me. Get this dress off me. I need you inside me."

"Tell me," he growled. "I want to hear you say it."

I closed my eyes, and another shudder rushed out with my breath. My eyes felt damp, and a tear rushed down my cheek. His thumb gently glided over the damp spot as he swiped it away. Then his mouth was by my ear once more.

"Ainsley Speire, I love you more than life itself." He leaned back and met my gaze.

I must have been wearing an expression of shock.

He chuckled and then continued. "I had no idea I needed you in my life until I finally saw you. *Really* saw you. Once you opened my eyes, my heart soon followed. Please, tell me you love me and your heart is mine for the taking. Please tell me you feel the same. I don't think I could take it if you didn't. But Ainsley, please, I need to know."

I stared into his eyes, the wonderment, the longing, the lust, and the love he felt for me radiating out of him. He spoke the truth. I could see it in the depths of his eyes. I felt my body shake again for a different reason. More tears slid down my cheeks.

I hiccupped and swiped at the wetness on my face. "As long as I've known you, Chase, I've wanted you in my life. I dreamed of being by your side, being your woman—hell, being your wife—for so long, and the first time you really saw me, because of that note, was the first day of my new life. There was no going back for me, not after that. I love you, Chase Newstrom, heart and soul. I love you."

In a flash, Chase released my hands and had his arms around my body. He lifted me into the air and held me close to him. I hugged my arms around his neck and brought my lips to his. Our tongues danced in a rhythm that met a perfect harmony. We were meant to be. I felt it. He felt it.

Chase carried me in the direction of my bedroom. Of course, we didn't make it that far.

"Ouch!" I yelled out when we bumped into the wall. I couldn't help laughing.

"Sorry about that," he said through his own laugh.

Once we made it to my bedroom, he set me on my feet and then took my hands once more and held them above my head.

"Don't move," he ordered.

I nodded.

He slid his hands down my arms and upper body until he reached the zipper of my dress. He pulled it down and helped me step out of it. He laid it across a sitting chair in my room and then returned to me. I stood in black panties, my stilettos, and my necklace and earrings but nothing else.

Chase took my hands and led me toward my bed, laid me down, and hovered over my body for a moment before slowly retreating. He stood, long and tall, his face filled with an emotion I could only describe as love. His eyes glistened, and he smiled down at me.

It wasn't every day anyone really had the privilege of knowing the real Chase Newstrom. He'd let his walls down for me and allowed me entrance to the most insecure parts of himself. I held the key to his heart and had no intention of tarnishing that trust.

He slipped his shirt off his shoulders and down his arms. His chest rose and fell with the breaths he took. His hair was slightly disheveled from the kissing we'd done against my door. He removed his pants, kicked off his shoes, and pulled off his socks. He stood in boxer briefs, and the outline of his erection pressed against the cotton material.

"Come here," I said and sat on the edge of my bed. He stepped forward, and I pulled at the waistline of his boxers, tugging them down his legs. His cock was mouth level with a small pearl of pre-come. I licked it and met his gaze.

Chase's mouth was slightly open, and he gasped when I licked him again. I wrapped my hand around his shaft and stroked him gently.

"Do you love me?" I asked. I knew the answer, but I wanted to play some after the very serious moment we'd just had.

He nodded and tucked hair that had fallen around my face behind my ear. "I love you."

I smiled and stroked him again. "I love you." I took him into my mouth and sucked on him, causing Chase to gasp once more. I took him in farther until he touched the back of my throat. He was large and so hard.

"I need to be inside you, baby," he groaned. "Let me have you."

I looked up his ripped stomach and pecs to meet his gaze. I gave his head a slight nibble, and he hissed. I licked him as if to soothe the burn.

"You *are* inside me."

"And it feels amazing, baby," he said and ran a hand under the back of my hairline. I then gasped when he fisted my hair. "I want to be fucking your pussy now."

My mouth was agape, and as he pulled my hair, he moved his other hand down between my legs. I separated them for him, and Chase moved my panties to the side. He pushed two fingers inside my pussy, and his thumb pressed against my clit. He moved his fingers against the sensitive flesh in a circular motion, awakening what could only be described as my inner beast.

The more he massaged the area, the more intense the feeling became, and my body thrashed on the bed. With his thumb teasing my clit, I was merely a ragdoll, and he was my puppet master.

He lowered himself to me, and his lips met mine in a force full of longing, need, and love. He pushed me to lie down on the bed, and his hand never wavered from the finger-fucking he was giving me. Chase let go of my hair and slid his hand down my neck to my breasts. He pinched the nipple on my left breast, and I hissed.

"Damn it," I groaned, sensing an orgasm building in the

lower part of my abdomen. I knew I would shatter very soon. "You're going to make me come before we even have sex." I licked my lips and met his gaze.

His eyes were hungry, and he looked as if he were about to devour me. And I was ready for the taking.

His free hand gripped the fabric of my barely there panties, and he ripped the material from my body. It was the most erotic thing anyone had ever done to me. He pushed my legs farther apart and placed his free hand just above the hood that covered my clit. He pulled my lower lips apart, and the cool of the air sent a jolt through my body just as Chase flicked his tongue against my already-swollen clit.

"Oh, shit," I gasped as I laid my head back on the bed. I reached above my head, grabbed the comforter, and pulled. I needed to hold on to something or my body may buck from the lashing Chase was giving my pussy. "Harder, please. I'm going to come. Harder!"

My clit throbbed, and my breaths became erratic as I panted. Chase sucked against my clit and nibbled.

And I shattered.

I screamed his name and my hips came off the bed. I wasn't sure when he stopped sucking and my body came back to the bed, but my chest rose and fell with the air I attempted to pull into my lungs. It was the most intense orgasm I had experienced in my life.

It was like skydiving. It wasn't the sensation of the air hitting your body but the spike of adrenaline and the euphoria your body felt as you were mid-climax.

I met his gaze after a moment, and a laugh pushed through my lips at the smirk that played on his face.

"You're welcome," he said and swiped his hand down his face.

CHASE

Ainsley lay before me, a goddess among women. Her pussy glistened with the aftermath of the orgasm I had just given her. The room had a slight chill, and her nipples had pebbled stiff. I reached forward and pinched one between my fingers. She smirked and lifted herself up to her elbows.

"A part of me wants to tie you up," I said, "and another part just wants to make love all night."

"It's almost midnight. Are you serious?"

I nodded. "Absolutely." I pulled her legs apart and yanked her toward me.

She squealed, followed by laughter. "Why not both?" she asked with a wicked gleam in her eyes.

I smirked and leaned down. I licked and pinched her nipple and then sucked on it for a moment. "Don't tease. Besides . . . " I glanced up at her from her breast as I switched to the other. "I didn't bring any rope with me." I sucked her other tit until I let it go with a pop. The head of my cock rubbed against her pussy. She was hot, wet, and ready.

I moved my hips against her, the friction of my dick rubbing directly on her clit. She gasped and ran her hands up the length of my arms. I continued to do this and relished the wetness her pussy left on my shaft.

Leaning down, I slanted my lips across hers. My tongue slid across her mouth, and she opened for me. I slid my tongue alongside hers as I continued rubbing myself against her. I was teasing her—not quite getting her off but more like light masturbation of our bodies. She moved her hips in rhythm with mine, and I fought the urge to slam myself balls deep.

"Fuck me, please," she whispered. "Stop teasing me and fuck me."

I grinned and licked her lips. "You want it, baby?"

She nodded, her mouth open as she gasped. "Yes, please."

I pulled back a little more, just enough to where the helmet of my cock pressed against the entrance to her pussy. As soon as I felt myself glide inside, I slammed down hard, pushing my full length inside her. She arched and yelled out my name, and her nails dug into my shoulders. I pulled back and thrust into her, harder than before.

She completely consumed me, and I was lost to this woman, lost to her body and soul. There was no life without her, and I couldn't remember anything before her. I had simply been breathing, but with Ainsley, I was alive.

I pushed into her over and over, my grunts growing louder with each thrust. She reached over her head and held on to something. The mattress? It didn't matter what she held on to Ainsley was mine.

"Mine," I groaned with a thrust. "You. Are. Mine."

"Yours," she gasped with a whimper. "I'm yours, always yours."

I pressed a palm to the bed and wrapped my free arm around her leg. I pushed it to her chest and drove farther into her. I needed more. I wanted all of her. Everything. It was as if I had been starving my entire life until I met Ainsley, my woman, my perfect match, my soul mate. She fulfilled me in every sense of the being.

My balls ached, and I knew my orgasm would happen soon. Too soon. I didn't want this to end.

"God, I could do this all night," I growled and pushed into her. "I want you all night, every night."

She giggled—not quite the response I was hoping for. I looked into her eyes, and she smiled up at me.

"Then I hope you bring some electrolytes and some lube, because we'll need it."

I chuckled and leaned down, bringing my lips to hers. "I love you," I whispered.

"I love you too."

"Oh, shit," I whispered, and I picked up my rhythm. "I'm going to come, baby. Come with me. Come now, Ainsley. Fuck, yes, come now!"

With a growl, I came. I slammed my cock hard into her, and she held on to my arms and yelled out my name. I felt her release as it mixed with my own. Sweat beaded on my forehead and trickled down my nose. I swiped it away and brought my forehead to hers.

"Ready for that glass of water?"

She grinned. "There's lube in my nightstand."

I chuckled and rolled off her. With my arm wrapped around her waist, I pressed my lips to her temple. "I love you, Ainsley Speire. More than words, more than anything."

She smiled and turned her head to face me. Her makeup had worn under her eyes, and her mascara ran. It only added to her beauty. "I love you a whole googolplex."

I blinked. "What is a googolplex?"

"It's the largest any number could ever possibly be," she explained. "It's like writing the number one with endless zeros."

"I had no idea, and now I love you a whole googolplex plus infinity."

She snorted. "That's so not a thing."

"Well." I chuckled. "It is now."

I held Ainsley in my arms for a few more minutes before I got out of bed and helped her to her feet. We showered, had sex before we left the bathroom, and then had to clean up again. I brought her water as promised, and she was ready on the bed, waiting patiently for me.

If I hadn't requested her to work the weekend of her best friend's wedding, she never would have drunk my Scotch and the note would never have been written.

Thank God I made her work that night.

EPILOGUE

AINSLEY

I stared at myself in the full-length mirror. My hair was pulled to the crown of my head in a braid of auburn hair. I had a few curls pulled down to frame my face. In front of my braid sat a tiara that held my veil.

My dress was sleeveless, strapless, and fitted to my waist. It flared in long satin and had a train behind it. My makeup was perfect, and I swore I would not cry.

"Come here, honey," my mother called. "Let me put some rouge on you."

"Mom, we call it lipstick in the twenty-first century."

She smeared the lipstick on my lips. "Smack your lips and make sure it spreads. I don't care what you kids call it. The color is beautiful on you. Take a look, darling."

I turned back to the mirror and smiled. She was right. The color was perfect. A bouquet of fresh roses, both white and red, were handed to me. I took them and looked at my sister, Everly. She had tears in her eyes, and she hugged me tight.

"I'm so proud of you," she whispered. "I knew he was the one."

I smiled and took a step back. "So, how do I look?"

"Like a knockout. He may break down and cry when he

sees you," she said. "In the best way possible, of course."

"Baby girl, are you ready?" my dad called.

My stomach fluttered with butterflies.

Chase had asked me to marry him on our one-year anniversary. He had moved me in with him, and I finally had met his mother. Some days were better than others when it came to her dementia. She was loving and kind. One day during a moment of clarity, she had told him, "Don't screw this one up, son. I like her!"

Coming back to the present, I looked at my father. "Yes, Daddy, I'm ready."

The music in the church began to play the wedding songs Chase and I had picked. My bridesmaid—and future sister-in-law and new best friend rolled into one—Madeline, made her way down the aisle, followed by my maid of honor, my sister. Once they were in place, the wedding march started, and everyone stood.

And down at the end of the walk stood my fiancé, Chase Newstrom.

CHASE

My eyes filled with tears, and I smiled so large it almost hurt. My heart beat loud enough I knew everyone in this place could hear it, even over the organ that played. But I didn't care. I would run into the street and confess my love of this woman, Ainsley Speire.

She made her way down the aisle with her father. Our eyes never wavered from each other. She smiled, and her red lips were beautiful under the light veil.

The night I asked Ainsley to marry me, we were walking

on the beach in Cozumel. I'd taken her on a vacation with me after another big case was won. We were hand-in-hand, barefoot in the sand. The sun was setting. It was perfect. I pulled her to a stop and kissed her. Then, I dropped to one knee, and she gasped and broke out in tears. She leaped into my arms screaming yes before I had the chance to ask her to marry me.

After we made love that night, I asked her while she lay in my arms. And she said yes.

"Do you take this man to be your lawfully wedded husband? To have and to hold, for better or worse, in sickness and in health, for richer or for poorer, till death do you part?"

Ainsley simply smiled and said, "I do."

The same question was repeated to me. I smiled and squeezed her hands. "I do."

"May I have the rings?" the preacher asked.

We handed them over, and one by one, we slipped them onto each other's fingers.

He said something else I didn't quite catch because as I stared into Ainsley's eyes, everything and everyone faded away.

"Son?" the preacher interrupted.

"Yes?" I answered.

"You may kiss your bride now."

A few in the church chuckled. We both apparently missed what he'd said. I lifted the veil that covered Ainsley, and underneath was the most beautiful woman in the world, my wife.

I took her into my arms, slanted my lips over hers, and kissed her. At that moment, my heart was full, so full it might burst. But I would have died a happy man.

I pulled away and looked into her eyes. "I love you, Mrs. Newstrom."

She giggled. "I love you too, Mr. Newstrom. And there's red lipstick all over your mouth."

I grinned, winked at her, and kissed her again.

Would Ainsley and I have ended up here today at our wedding? I would like to think so. Regardless, we were here now, and that was all I needed in this world of misadventures with Scotch, love notes, and my Ainsley.

ACKNOWLEDGMENTS

Thank you to my readers who have stuck by me through this whirlwind adventure in writing! I wouldn't be here without your support. And for that, I'll be forever grateful.

Thank you to the Waterhouse team, especially to Meredith Wild and Scott Saunders. You two are amazing!

To my street team, you guys are fantastic! Thank you for everything you do! I love y'all!

MORE MISADVENTURES

**VISIT MISADVENTURES.COM
FOR MORE INFORMATION!**

ABOUT THE AUTHOR

USA Today and award-winning bestselling author Julie Morgan holds a degree in computer science and loves science fiction shows and movies. Encouraged by her family, she began writing. Originally from Texas, Julie now resides in central Florida with her husband and daughter, where she is an advocate for children with special needs. She can be found playing games with her daughter when she isn't lost in another world.

Visit her at www.JulieMorganBooks.com